FOR YOU
TO SEE
THE STARS

BE SURE AND PICK UP:

FOR YOU TO SEE THE STARS
A companion CD of songs behind the stories
Radney Foster
(Devil's River Records)
Available at radneyfoster.com and your favorite
independent record store

ALSO BY RADNEY FOSTER

Del Rio, Texas 1959

Labor of Love

See What You Want to See

Are You Ready for the Big Show?

Another Way to Go

And Then There's Me (The Back Porch Sessions)

This World We Live In

Revival

Del Rio, Texas Revisited

Everything I Should Have Said

A COLLECTION OF STORIES

FOR YOU
TO SEE
THE STARS

by radney foster

Working Title Farm

an imprint of River's Edge Media

FOR YOU TO SEE THE STARS
Copyright © 2017 by Radney Foster.

Working Title Farm
6834 Cantrell Road, Suite 172
Little Rock, AR 72207

Edited by Shari Smith and Judy Richards

Cover design: Cary Smith
Cover illustration: Cyndi Hoelzle

For You to See the Stars/Radney Foster—1st ed.
ISBN 978-1-940595-64-1 (Hardback)
ISBN 978-1-940595-65-8 (Softback)
ISBN 978-1-940595-66-5 (ebook))
Printed in the United States of America

For Cyndi, you believe

CONTENTS

FOREWORD

The bus was an old Eagle. She was painted dark green and had a modified top just above the cab to make her more aerodynamic but no prettier. They don't make Eagles anymore but for me nothing ever sailed smoother. The suspension rocked more front to back than side to side and that was her magic. You could crawl into your bunk exhausted but still wired from the adrenalin rush of a sweat soaked show, and read 'til that Eagle, in the hands of Dan Gillis, rocked you to sleep. Dan owned her and drove as fine as anyone who ever put a hand to the wheel.

I was twenty-seven years old, in a band with Bill Lloyd, and we believed that if we didn't leave every ounce of who we were on that stage we were doing it wrong. I have scars on my knuckles and bloodstains on a Gibson to prove it. We did it night after night, playing country music as hard as the Clash played rock and roll.

I thought I was a reader before I hit the road, but I was a novice. Two hundred and seventeen nights in one year with a band on a bus will either make you a real reader or crazy ... maybe a little of both. I had seen every VHS tape in the bus five times, hell, I had *Raising Arizona* memorized. There were no cell phones, no iPads. But I did have books to cure the soul-numbing boredom of rolling down the interstate from Amarillo to Davenport to Saskatoon and I shared them with my bandmates.

Reading made me a better songwriter. Mary Martin, my first A & R rep at RCA had a sign on her office door that said, "If you don't read you can't write." I didn't truly understand that 'til after my first year on the road. When Bill and I first wrote with Guy Clark that year he talked about Picasso, Paris, Conroy, Hemingway, and Hatch green chiles. Dozens of backstage discussions with my heroes made me realize it was a fine thing to write and perform a hit song but what I was really after was art. When a hit falls from the chart, the artistry is what is remembered.

We lost Guy last year. I miss him.

I spent the next twenty-eight years writing songs that might touch a heart and make someone care, not about me but about their own lives, loves, successes, and failures. In the process they would ask how I got a peek inside their living room, inside their heart. Maybe they'd buy a record or even a ticket to a show. It's made me a living creating characters, mining my own hopes and disappointments, and wrapping them around a melody. I played damn near every honky-tonk, coffee house, hippie festival, and county fair in this country and along the way always had a book.

In November of 2015 I got sick, so sick that I completely lost my voice for over a month. I had to cancel a lot of shows. I coughed through Christmas and could only communicate by writing notes. Losing your voice for that long is an existential crisis for a singer. I had a Come-to-Jesus moment while stoned on cough medicine.

What if I can't ever sing again? What do I do for a living? Who am I?

I am a storyteller.

How can I tell stories if I can't sing?

I wrote a note to my wife that I was going to write a story based on a new song. It would help with my boredom and worry.

"Hallelujah! You should. You're driving me crazy."

In the living room watching the snow fall outside my front window that January I wrote "Sycamore Creek." Cyndi was a magazine editor and a writer for many years. I was more nervous handing her that story than turning in a song to any music publisher in my entire career. She told me that it was good. Really good.

"Babe, you need to keep writing even after you get your voice back."

About a year and a half dozen stories later, I got a call from Shari Smith. Our mutual friend Mary Gauthier suggested she call me about writing a song for Shari's book, art, and music project *Trio*. I told Shari I'd be happy to write a song for Brian Panowich's great novel *Bull Mountain*. I mentioned to Shari that I also wrote short fiction and would she consider reading something I'd written. "Sure … that would be fine."

I could hear the dread. Shari would make a terrible poker player.

Two days later, my phone rang. "Gotdamn, Radney Foster, you can write a pretty sentence." Shari cusses a lot. "But you're hiding the pretty." I told her I didn't quite understand but was willing to learn. We talked a long time about my idea of a book of short fiction to go along with my next record and I sent her another story and then another.

One night after supper, Shari texted me a couple things she thought I should read. "Call me when you are done. I want to talk about one of your stories." I did as she asked and steeled myself with a bourbon on my back porch.

I called and she read something she'd written in the style of the other stories. I laughed out loud, was completely sucked in through the whole thing, and cried like a baby at the end. Shari told me to open up one of my stories on my computer and go to page 4, second paragraph. "Read it to me." I did. "Now Radney, that is as fine as anything I've read. So you tell me why it's buried on the fourth page. And buddy, if you can write a paragraph that pretty you gotta write 'em all that pretty. Go to work."

Within a week I'd rewritten that story and Shari had offered me a publishing deal with Working Title Farm. I didn't want to work with anyone else. The result is this compilation of short stories and the songs that inspired them or vice versa.

Take your pick.

For You to See the Stars

The package was not large or heavy but it was a burden. Whatever my father's intentions had been in having me deliver it were beyond my comprehension. I had no idea what was inside and had strict instructions not to open it. I loved my father and it was my duty to see this journey through but I knew that he was making mischief from beyond the grave.

The plane touched down and it jarred me from a deep, exhausted sleep. I felt those brief seconds of peaceful ignorance, those first waking moments of simply being before remembering that my father was dead. *Daddy's gone.* I blew out a breath and the physical sorrow that follows death laid down next to my soul and began gnawing at me again.

The pilot announced that it was 102 degrees outside, could be even hotter before the day was over. "Welcome to El Paso." A groan went up from the passengers. I fumbled through my duffel bag to find my phone and called my mother as I left the plane.

"Mama?"

"Beau? Whatcha doin', sweetie?"

"I'm getting off a plane in El Paso. I'm about to …"

She cut me off. "For the life of me, I don't know why you don't just mail that goddamn thing. This is your daddy steppin' into my business that I wouldn't let him touch for almost twenty years. I wish you would do as I asked and just mail it! He only gave it to you to …" I could hear the tears and I waited, knowing that talking to her would do no good. She sighed and said, "I miss him so much …. It has been thirty-seven days and I've cried every one. He was such a good man and was everything to me but he loved a joke and I swear this is one of his crazy jokes! I hate it that he's brought you into it."

"Mama, he asked me to do this because I'm his oldest son. Daddy was real specific."

The letter had been clear. It hadn't been written in haste or the grief of knowing he would die soon. His death was sudden, a heart attack with no foreshadowed diagnosis. He had written the instructions in a letter directly to me and left it with his law partner, Sam Harding. Sam delivered the letter and whatever the hell I was now carrying the day after Daddy died. Apparently, the item had lived in my father's law desk.

"Beau, I'm just scared of what this might stir up."

"I know, but it feels like the right thing to do. He asked me to do it this way. So, I'm driving down to Alpine and I'll let you know more soon…. I love you, Mama."

"I love you, too, Beau."

"Mama?"

"Yes?"

"I miss him, too … all the time. I promise I'll call."

It is a long way to the mountains of far West Texas, and no matter where you come from there is no closest major airport. You'll be driving several hours at 85 or 90 miles per hour no matter where you land. I was not prepared for the distances. The beauty of the desert mountains overwhelmed me.

As I drove south, the sand grays and yellows turned to bright green. I flew past grass prairies studded with crazy flowering cacti, bushes that looked like the Devil's walking stick, and something akin to the agave plants I'd seen on tequila labels. Antelope grazed as the late afternoon sun turned the mountains and mesas into purple shadows with red and gold flares of light in the folds of the hillsides; such beauty in a place so desolate.

There was a quirkiness to the people out here long before there were galleries in Marfa, much less a Prada storefront as an art piece in the middle of nowhere. These rugged mountains and deserts may be beautiful, but it is rough country and those who choose it as home do not do so lightly. There are too many other places easier to live. My mother's family was from this area, but when she married my father she adopted Mobile with its softer edges and accents. I had last been out here when I was eight years old for my grandmother's funeral.

I pulled into the motel in Alpine at sunset and was surprised by how cool it was outside. I fished a denim shirt out of my duffel bag and walked to the front desk to check in. The desk clerk gave me instructions on how to turn on the heat.

"Heat?"

"You're at 4,500 feet, son. It might be in the 40s by morning."

I tossed my stuff in my room and headed to the one contact I had here, at a bar and restaurant called the Saddle Club. The place was packed, which reminded me it was Friday night. I squeezed up to the only space at the bar and asked the pretty blonde bartender for a beer. She was poured into jeans and a black leather western vest with silver concho buttons, her purple and black lace push-up bra peeking out from underneath. She smiled, leaned her cleavage against the bar, and said, "Frat boy, the Sul Ross coeds are down the street, where they sell beer in plastic cups and don't look too close at your fake ID."

I pulled out my New York driver's license. "I'm a baby face

but I'm twenty-six. I'm looking for Umberto Nuñez. I think he's a manager here?" She looked at the ID and laughed. "That's got to be real 'cause none of the cowboys around here would be smart enough to pull off faking a New York license. Plus they'd be scared they'd get their ass kicked." I raised an eyebrow and grinned. "I'm just kiddin' ya," she said. "Rebecca." She stuck her hand out to shake. "Who you lookin' for again?"

"Umberto Nuñez"

"Umm who? Nuñez?" Her eyes got wide. She smiled and out shot, "Oh, shit, Bucky! Umberto! I never knew his real first name." She laughed and stomped her foot. "Baby face James from New York, you just gave me all kinds of ammunition to tease his ass. The beer is on me. He's here but it might be a while. He's swamped in the kitchen on account of we're short a cook tonight. He's gonna be stuck back there 'til the dinner rush is gone. Umberto, hot damn! Here, have a Shiner Bock. It's a Texas thing."

After another beer and dinner, a short man who looked to be in his mid-forties with black hair cut military style and dark eyes walked out of the kitchen sweating and drinking from a huge plastic cup of iced tea. His neck and shoulders were roped up as if he were a body builder or a Marine sergeant. Rebecca pointed at me. He smiled and said, "Howdy. Bucky Nuñez. What can I do you for?"

"I'm looking for Joaquin Garrison. I, uh have …"

"If you're lookin' to learn how to rodeo, he don't do that no more. If you need a well witched I can get in touch with him tomorrow."

"Well witched?"

"Yea, you know, find where the water is closest to the surface so you don't have to drill damn near to China and waste thousands of dollars. He's a water witch. If that ain't why you're here, he's probably not gonna see ya. He's kind of a recluse."

"I'm his grandson."

He stood there slack jawed for a second, then grabbed a bar towel, wiped his forehead, and said, "I'll … be … damned.

You favor him, now that I think about it. Wow! Does he know you're comin'?"

"No sir, you are the only contact I have for him. I've got no phone number and he doesn't email. I've got to deliver something to him from …" I took a swig of beer and swallowed hard. "My father passed away and wanted me to give him a package."

His eyes lost their brightness. They did not change voluntarily but in the way that only someone who had experienced death would react. "Oh man … I'm sorry for your loss, son. I'm real sorry to hear that. I met your Dad once a long time ago in Ft. Stockton before you were born. He was a nice guy."

He leaned back on a beer bin and we sat there in our own silence with the cacophony of the restaurant weaving around us. Finally he said, "Look, I don't want to be rude but I'll need to call Joaquin in the mornin' and ask him what he wants to do. There's only two people in the whole damn world that have he and Susanna's number, me and a woman named Kate Richards in Marfa. Joaquin will skin my ass if I give it out. Where ya stayin'?"

"At the Maverick Inn."

"Oh and hell, I'm sorry, I don't even know your name."

"James. James Garrison Smallwood." We shook hands, exchanged numbers, and he asked if I could meet him for breakfast around nine the next morning. He refilled his iced tea and said he needed to get back to work. As he was headed back to the kitchen he called across the room, "Rebecca, his dinner and drinks are on me." She called back, "Sure thing, Umberto!"

He stopped in his tracks, his head slumped to his chest. He shook it slowly back and forth, blew out a breath of resignation, and continued into the kitchen. She winked at me and we both laughed.

I woke up early the next morning cold, dehydrated, and fumbled with the thermostat to turn on the heat. I drank water and made a cup of coffee hoping to cure my headache. *I've gotta buy a sweatshirt or a jacket.*

I sat in the cold stillness of dawn, watching the light change out my window, saddled with the emptiness of losing my father, not so much crying or sobbing but feeling the uncontrollable tears roll down my face. After more than a month of him gone, I was sick of not being able to talk to him like I had almost daily when he was alive. I resolved then and there to not stop talking to him, even if he was in the next world. I would just get my answers differently.

What is this trip about, Dad?

I was starving by the time Bucky called at 8:30 and said to meet at a Mexican food place in half an hour. In my restlessness I had already run three miles through town, worked out, showered, and shaved. I got there first, sat down, and ordered. Bucky walked in and greeted everyone in the joint, coaxing smiles and laughter from corner to kitchen. He asked if I'd ordered yet and I told him I had, coffee and a burrito. He barked a series of instructions to the waitress in Spanish. She shook her head and laughed. Bucky turned to me and said, "You don't want that. You want the special. Trust me. I ordered you the pork green chile enchiladas with two fried eggs on top."

I could not help but laugh.

"You are like the mayor or something. Is there anyone you don't know around here?" Then I smiled and added, "Or tell what to eat for breakfast?"

He laughed. "Alpine isn't very big, plus that waitress is my niece. I can take you to Joaquin and Susanna's after breakfast. Are you in a car or a truck?

"Some kind of GM rental car."

"You are never gonna get there in that, plus I doubt you could find it unless you have a high dollar GPS. It's a couple hours away. I can take you, but I can't stay. Joaquin has a well to witch this afternoon and wants you to go with him. Susanna has to go to Marfa on Monday and can drop you on the way. So you might be out there a couple of days."

"Wow, how far away do they live?"

"It's only seventy miles, but thirty of it are gravel ranch road, and the last five are up a mountain. It's beautiful out there but there's no calling an Uber if you get bored. There's no cell service at all. Joaquin and Susanna make everything slow down ... but in a good way. You good with that?"

"I suppose I'll have to be. I haven't seen my granddad since I was a kid and I don't even know who Susanna is. Is she his wife?"

The enchiladas came and the waitress set down two bowls of salsa, green and red. Bucky popped the yolks on the fried eggs and put green salsa on one egg and red on the other. "Careful with the green stuff, it'll bite ya." I followed his lead. As he blew on his first bite to cool it, he said, "OK, the short answer is no, she's not his wife, but she's been with him a long, long time .... I don't think they give a care about the piece of paper. Come to think of it, there's not a whole lot of conventions they adhere to, period. I can fill you in some in the truck on the way but I think you need to learn this stuff from them. You should ask them all the questions in the world. They both like telling stories. They've kind of created their own crazy world out there and it's one of the coolest houses I've ever seen."

I must have looked strange while I tried to process all this, because he laughed and said, "Hey don't worry, they're not really crazy, just eccentric ... but they are true hearted people. There was a time in my life when no one gave a damn about me but Joaquin, and I'll never forget it."

After breakfast, I called Mama to tell her what was happening and not to worry if she didn't hear from me for a few days. Thankfully she didn't answer and I left a message. I checked out of the motel, bought a jacket and a Sul Ross State sweatshirt, then met Bucky in the parking lot of the Saddle Club. We headed south toward Big Bend National Park and turned on a gravel road after an hour, then drove another hour up into the desertous mountains gaining elevation all the way. The last fifteen minutes were a buckle-up, four-wheel-drive thrill ride to match anything

Disneyland could offer. Bucky pointed out ranches, mesas, and old battle sites between Buffalo Soldiers and Indians. I listened to him, the rattle of the dually truck, and my own thoughts 'til we arrived.

You ever been out here, Dad? Come out here and not tell Mama? Why are you doing this? I sure hope this whole thing makes sense.

The house was adobe, ancient, and crooked, framed by green cactus and rock gray mountains behind it. The walls were the yellow of the spruce top on a Martin guitar turning to rose in the sunset. The window and doorframes had been painted a bright blue once upon a time but were graying. There was a bench to the left of the door with a half dozen or more pots of desert flowers and a few tools artfully stacked at one end. On the other side of the door was a Bill Worrell sculpture inspired by a six-thousand-year-old Native American pictograph.

I turned around to pull my duffel from the back of the truck and the view stopped me. You could see the whole of the southern Rockies as they wove their way south into Mexico, cut through the middle by the waters of the Rio Grande.

"It takes your breath away doesn't it, son."

I turned back and saw my grandfather behind me looking out at the view. He was tall, gray headed, and every bit the cowboy from head to toe. Not the dressed-up-for-the-rodeo kind but a real cowboy whose weathered clothes matched his skin. He smiled. His green eyes were kind and I immediately saw my mother in them.

"Don't let me interrupt you. That vista is a fine thing to linger over … it never stops changing."

"Granddad! I … uh … you …"

"It's been too long, James. You grew up on me."

I reached out to shake hands and felt the awkwardness of the missing years. He shook my hand for a long while, then said, "You look to be a fine young man and we have a lot of catching up to do. Come on in the house. We'll start by meeting Susanna."

We walked into a low-ceilinged great room with wood beams

and French doors on the opposite side. The room was cool and dark but inviting. There was a large fireplace at one end and an open kitchen at the other. The white adobe walls, bookshelves, side tables, mantle, and even the floor were covered by an eclectic mix of art and artifacts. A well-oiled old saddle, a Gustave Baumann wood block print, wrought-iron crosses, Hopi and Pueblo Indian pots, an Ansel Adams photo, board games, a trilobite fossil, a pair of silver spurs, books on art and history, novels, modern art collages, charcoal sketches of nudes and still lifes, and a painting by Elena Hernandez-Gaelyn cluttered the house. Their placement was no accident, each thing complementing its neighbor.

The French doors were open to a patio with a wood-framed trellis covered by a cedar-stick lattice providing dappled shade. I could smell some type of jasmine and see the flowers in the vines that climbed the posts. I could also hear Bucky and a woman's voice laughing and speaking in Spanish outside. A dog bounded in and looked at me, wanting attention. My grandfather petted the dog and said, "This is Jackie, the other woman in my life."

"Joaquin?" a woman's voice called as she entered the room.

She was quite possibly the most beautiful woman I had ever met. She had brown wavy hair tied loosely with red, white, and green ribbons in a ponytail, and her dark almond-shaped eyes were filled with delight. Her oval face, brown skin, and high cheekbones marked her of Native American and Spanish ancestry. I knew she had been with my grandfather for more than fifteen years but could not tell her age. I assumed somewhere between forty and sixty, but if she'd told me she was thirty-five, I'd have believed her. She was wearing a white blouse and had a multicolored sash at her waist above a pale green flower-patterned traditional Mexican flowing skirt, with three deep green ribbons that matched the ones in her hair and circled just above the hem. She was barefoot on the clay-tiled floor. She came toward me, grabbed my shoulders, and kissed both my cheeks, which disarmed me. "Joaquin and I are so happy you are here, James.

I am sad about the circumstances that brought you but overjoyed to meet you." She offered iced tea and said we would all eat on the patio before it got too hot. Bucky politely bowed out and said he had to get back to town. Joaquin said, "We better hurry. I've got a well to witch at 3 o'clock."

We ate posole, a pork and hominy stew with fresh radish slices, cabbage, avocado, and pico de gallo. I had never been a hominy fan and was shocked at its deliciousness. They pumped out question after question about my life, wanting to soak up as much knowledge about me, my brother, sister, and of course my mother. They wanted to know how I'd gotten from Mobile, Alabama, to New York and where I'd developed my interest in art, architecture, and design. As we were taking dishes to the kitchen, my grandfather said, "James, I'm so sorry about your daddy. He truly loved your mother, and I knew he would be good to her from the first time I met him.

"The last several years have been strained between your mama and me, but I'm not telling you anything you don't already know."

His eyes glistened and he stopped. Susanna came up next to him and pulled his arm over her shoulder. She said, "Let us show you your room."

They took me down the hall to a small bedroom with a round adobe fireplace built into the corner. It was laid with paper, kindling, and wood in case it was cold that night. On the far wall was an acrylic, charcoal, and collage painting by Njideka Akunyili Crosby.

My grandfather told me they were going to take a siesta and then he had to go to work. "Son, would you want to ride over there with me? I'll understand if you're too tired and want to stay here."

"No, I'd love to go. Just let me know when you're ready." I decided to lie down, and in what seemed like seconds, my grandfather was gently jostling my shoulder. It had been close to an hour and I'd slept so hard I was completely disoriented. He said

I didn't have to go if I needed rest. "No, no … just let me splash my face and I'm ready to go." He said he'd meet me outside.

Daddy, when do I tell 'em about the package? Will it hurt them? They seem happy. Will it hurt Mama if I give it to Joaquin?

Joaquin and I rode for an hour on a different route to the same highway I came in on, but hit it further south, and then on more back roads to a plot of land on a hillside. My grandfather was quiet mostly, and his demeanor and economy of words when he did speak let me know that, like me, he was not uncomfortable with silence. I was riding with a stranger but I was riding with kin.

I could see a half dozen houses in the distance. We met a real estate agent named Ben Stegler, acting for some landowner from Dallas building a house on this twenty-acre "ranchito."

"Hey Ben, this is my grandson James from New York." Joaquin half shouted over the wind. We shook hands and traded greetings all around. Ben kicked a clod of caliche and said, "Joaquin, I know you don't like this … these folks have two house sites in mind. One is marked at the top of this rise and if you look south towards the road when you get there, the other is marked on the flat about a hundred and fifty yards away."

"It's alright, Ben, you caught me on a good day. I'll give you two well sites and the second one is half price. I'm gonna start walking. James, would you mind hanging back with Ben? I need to concentrate."

He put on his cowboy hat and walked west toward a group of marked stakes at the top of the hill, slow and steady, as if preoccupied by his thoughts. Ben pulled two stakes with green tape and a hammer out of the back of his Suburban. We followed my grandfather, keeping our distance. I turned to Ben and said, "You are both serious about this. I mean no disrespect, but this seems a little like snake oil."

"Son, all I know is when I convince a client to hire Joaquin, they tend to find water with better pressure and several hundred feet shallower. That saves them thousands of dollars. The six hundred bucks I'm paying today feels like pretty good insurance. He believes ... so I believe."

"I was surprised he didn't pull out a forked stick or something, like in the movies."

Ben laughed, "That's the snake oil! If the landowner were here, Joaquin would size them up. If they seem like they need the visual, he's got some cool looking sticks in the back of the truck."

My grandfather found the first site after twenty minutes and then the second half an hour later. He then explained the pluses and minuses of each to Ben. The second site would need to drill deeper. The landowner could always drill up top and pipe the water down. Ben wrote out the check. As Joaquin and I drove off, I asked, "How do you know where it is? The water I mean."

"A little knowledge of topography and geology doesn't hurt, but like most things in life it still boils down to faith. I believe the water is singing to me. Wherever she sings the prettiest, I tell them to drill there."

We drove in silence for another half hour and then my grandfather asked, "James, how long ago did your Daddy pass?"

"May ninth, a little over a month ago. How did you and Susanna know before I got here?"

"Bucky told me when he called. Does your mama know you are here?"

"Yes sir, she does ... but she's not happy about it."

He laughed out loud. "No, I imagine she's not. Catherine is still Catherine. We'll talk more about that later ... tonight after dinner. Do you like bourbon? We'll drink a toast to your dad. Sometimes bourbon eases a hard conversation."

"Yes sir, I like bourbon. I *am* from Mobile."

He laughed again. "Tell me about your sister, Kristen. Is she still at Tulane? And you have a brother I've never met, Jefferson. Tell me all about them."

I looked at him for a long moment. *How does he keep up even though we don't?* I began to tell him all about Kristen and Jefferson,

Tulane and high school, likes and dislikes, adventures and mishaps. He soaked it all up as we rattled over rocky ranch roads home.

When we arrived and walked back into the cool adobe house, Susanna came in through the patio doorway wearing a thin white cotton nightgown speckled with paint. The garment was gauzy and sunlight silhouetted her naked body underneath. I could not help but stare and then turn away in my embarrassment. She giggled and said, "Oops, I was painting and forgot myself. I'll just go change." Joaquin walked in behind me and laughed, realizing what had happened. "You'll have to forgive both Susanna and I ... we don't generally have house guests. There's beer in the fridge. I'm gonna clean up for dinner." He headed back to their bedroom and I could hear laughter and conversation from down the hall. It was a lover's conversation, and I knew enough to grab a beer and go to the patio out of earshot. On an easel was the beginnings of a painting, of a woman carrying a child in the desert.

We had dinner on the patio in the rose light of sunset. "You have an amazing home and a beautiful collection of art here," I said. "It's so eclectic but it all fits together, you can tell the pieces all mean something to you. Is that a Hernandez-Gaelyn painting in the living room? I saw some of her works in Chicago once at an exhibit of contemporary Latina artists."

They both stopped eating and stared at me in silence. Then they burst into laughter. Joaquin began to cough, he was laughing so hard. I was dumbstruck by their reaction. Susanna sensed my discomfort, calmed her laughter, and spoke while wiping the tears away. "I am Susanna Elena Hernández-Gaelyn. That painting is the only one your grandfather won't let me sell. It's the first thing I painted when we moved in here together fifteen or more years ago. The fact that you even know who I am is a great compliment."

I began to rub my forehead with one hand, closed my eyes, and laughed.

"I'd like to propose a toast," I said as I raised my wine glass, "to artists and idiots. God help us all." Joaquin laughed and said, "Don't be too hard on yourself, son."

After supper it was time to do what I came to do. Joaquin lit a fire in the chimenea and Susanna brought out a bottle of Woodford's, three glasses, and a bowl of ice. I excused myself and brought the package from the bedroom and sat across from my grandfather and his lover by the fire. *This is harder than I thought it would be, Dad.* I took a deep breath and a sip of whiskey. "I don't know what to say ... but here goes. When Daddy died, he had left some instructions in his will and one was for me to hand deliver this to you, Granddad. I have no idea what it is."

"Well, let's see what's inside." He carefully took out a pocket-knife and cut open the tape that held the box closed. Inside was a letter in an envelope and a smaller white box that was nested in packing paper as if the box were holy. He sliced open the letter and stood to get more light from the string of Christmas lights that lit the patio to read the single typed page. Tears began to well in his eyes and then stream silently down his face. He put the letter in the fire, said, "Y'all excuse me," and walked into the house without opening the small white box. Susanna followed and I heard the front door open. I decided it was best to stay put.

Dad, what have we done? Have you and I just poured salt in the wound? Damn, I wish someone would explain what the hell happened. What the hell killed something between this man and Mama?

Susanna finally walked back out on the patio with a jacket. She gave me matter-of-fact instructions. "Put on this jacket, take your bourbon and Joaquin's. Walk out front. It's dark out there, he's a ways out ... let your eyes adjust."

Heading out the front door, I understood her caution. There were no lights on the front of the house and no lights visible anywhere on the entire vista save one to the southwest, a lone escaped star from the sea of them overhead. I had never seen anything like it. How long had this view of the heavens been here challenging the ego of humans, a beauty so vast and breathtaking it made us paint, sing, pray, search, or just rest in the awe of its vastness? I walked a few more yards out into the black and finally broke the silence. "Granddad? Joaquin?"

"I'm another ten yards in front of you. Be careful getting here."

"I brought your whiskey. The stars are amazing. I've never seen so many."

"There's no light pollution, except for that one ranch house fifteen miles south. They'll turn those off after a while."

I stood in silence with my grandfather and took a sip of bourbon. This moment was his as well as mine and I began to feel the ache of missing my father.

Finally, Joaquin broke the silence. "It's gotta get dark enough for you to see the stars. Really see them. It's one of the reasons Susanna and I came here. I've only ever been one other place where you could see them like this ... Alaska. I worked there when your mama was a baby, after I got back from Vietnam. Did you know she was born while I was in Vietnam?"

"No sir."

"So much catching up to do. I'm gonna start with your grandma. Do you have any memory of her death? Coming to her funeral?"

"A little. I was eight."

"My sweet Emily. She was the light of my life ... we were high school sweethearts and got married when I was drafted, before I went to 'Nam. Catherine was our only child. That made her the center of attention."

I grinned. "Mama still likes being the center of attention." Joaquin laughed and then quieted.

"When your grandma died of cancer, your mama and I grieved in different ways. She wanted me closer. I, on the other hand, crawled in a bottle of this brown liquor, lost my hardware business in Ft. Stockton, sold my house, and wandered the West. Your mama kept wanting me to move to Mobile so she could straighten me out. And then I met Susanna in Taos." He took a sip of whiskey. "Falling in love with a Mexican bohemian painter younger than she was, a year after her mother had died, was more than Catherine could handle. I don't think she thought it would last. She couldn't understand that my loving Susanna didn't diminish my love for, or memory of, her mama. We were just grieving in different ways but it broke something in Catherine and I was too stubborn to figure out how to fix it.

"After a few years, the separation was just how life was." He paused. "I'm sorry for that, son. I'm sorry because I lost out on being a part of your life, your brother's and your sister's, too." He killed his whiskey and said, "Let's go back to the fire. It's chilly and I have more to tell you."

We walked in the house and Susanna hugged him. He leaned down and kissed her and said, "I love you." There were tears in her eyes. She ushered us to the fire. I was offered more whiskey but declined.

As we sat down I said, "You haven't opened the smaller box."

Joaquin said, "I already know what it is … I'd like you to have it. It's what your father wanted. It's why he sent you here. Open it."

I looked at the box and didn't know what to think, but slowly picked it up out of its nest and opened it. Inside was a gold pocket watch with a heavy chain. The watch had a white face and Arabic numerals. The letters JGS were engraved on the back. I stared at the beautiful antique and finally said, "But … I don't understand."

My grandfather reached out and I handed him the watch. "When John married your mama, I felt like I gained a son I'd never had. They had dated all the while she was at Tulane and I had grown to love him. I wasn't afraid or angry, like most fathers, walking my daughter down the aisle to him. Something about him gave your mama peace. The watch is a railroad watch, thus the Arabic numerals. It had been my father's, who worked as an engineer for Southern Pacific. I gave it to your dad the night before their wedding day. I had his initials engraved on it …. I believe those are your initials as well. It's only right that you should have it. I think your dad thought if anything happened to him I should give it to you if I was still alive. He was very thoughtful that way. He's wanted me to reconcile with your mama a long time ... you and that watch are his final attempt. I think he knew enough about us both that we would form a bond if you came out here."

"How do you know that he wanted you to reconcile?"

"I have something else to show you."

He got up and went in the house. I heard a lock unbolt. He came back with a shoebox and took the top off. It was filled with letters. Joaquin tipped it toward me and slowly raked his thumb across the tops so I could see my father's law office letterhead, Johnson, Smallwood and Harding. "Your father wrote me twice a year, every year since Emily died. I'd get a letter just before Christmas and on May 27, the anniversary of her death. I lied a little when I said I got out of Bucky that your daddy had passed. I knew something was wrong when I'd not heard from him by the first of June. Bucky only confirmed it.

"Your father kept me up to date with all of you, your lost teeth, grades, sports, swimming lessons, mishaps, everything. I would write him back at his office and thank him, so your mother wouldn't get angry."

I slumped back in my chair, closed my eyes, and began to bawl. I couldn't understand why. I just knew I missed my father more than ever. My grandfather patted my leg and got up to give me space. Susanna followed him and kissed the top of my head as they went into the house to do the dishes.

After I had cried myself empty of tears I walked to the doorway, leaned against it, and said, "I think I'll take you up on that second whiskey."

Susanna said, "Help yourself." Joaquin asked, "Would you like our company or do you need more time alone?"

"Can I ask more questions?"

Joaquin said, "Ask all you like. Stay here as long as you like.

You are my grandson, James, and my prayer is you are the river that guides me back to my family."

We walked back out and Susanna put another log in the chimenea as Joaquin poured me another bourbon. I sat down and asked, "Why did you burn the letter?"

"Your father told me to."

"What did it say?"

"Everything it needed to."

Dear Joaquin,
It's time. Show him the stars. Give him the watch. Burn this letter.
See you across the Jordan.
John

Listen to "For You to See the Stars," from the album
For You to See the Stars by Radney Foster.

Bridge Club

In 1963, Bridge Club was holy. It was mentioned in reverential tones, the way one spoke of church on Easter Sunday or of University of Texas football. Bridge Club ladies arrived in as much Jackie Kennedy style as their provincial pocketbooks could manage. Their red lipstick, poufy hair, sleek dresses, Italian purses, and sometimes even white gloves were more important than who won the game. All that finery was purchased at Frost's in San Antonio or perhaps Neiman's in Dallas and driven home to West Texas in station wagons. Bridge Club was a religious ritual with vestments.

Rituals are important. They bind us. Families pass them down, generation to generation. The way my family prays at the dinner table or that I am forevermore elated by time spent in nature were gifts given to me by my folks. My father knew that catching crawdads in the irrigation ditch would lead to hiking in National Parks with him and later with my own children. But as much as my mother tried, many times, to teach me the game of bridge, it never took.

The DNA required to appreciate the elegance of a silver coffee set was not passed down to me but the pull of the outdoors is in my blood. My feet were muddy from my first steps.

One of my earliest memories as a child was of my father teaching me to pee in the backyard. It was my first rite of passage and is as important as Confirmation, going fishing, learning to shoot a gun, high school graduation, and touching a girl's breasts for the first time.

If you are busy in the backyard being Superman, the Green Lantern, or the Lone Ranger, going to the bathroom is a waste of time. There are so many other grand adventures you could be having. Playing with Matchbox cars, being a pirate on a swing set, or running through the sprinkler were all much more important than peeing. At three and a half it was not worth thinking about until I had to go so bad that wide-eyed fear overtook me. I then had to run into the house, close the door so Mama wouldn't get mad, walk with my legs closed together down the hall, open and close the door to the bathroom, remember to lift the toilet seat, wriggle my pants down, and finally aim correctly in the toilet. Doing all of this without wetting myself, or the bathroom floor, was dang near impossible.

The day my father told me that I could just unzip my britches and go on one of the three large shade trees in our backyard was as miraculous an experience as Moses receiving those ancient tablets of stone. He was planting tomatoes and I was helping by playing in the water and the dirt. When I started dancing around he knew immediately what was up. "Son, you can go and pee on that big pecan tree and then come back and help me finish."

"Mama won't get mad?"

"No, just be sure and wash up when you go inside. We'll remind you." I ran over to that pecan, took good aim, and hit it with a great deal of satisfaction.

My father then told me that if I was playing outside and needed to go and didn't have time to get to the bathroom, I could always run behind one of the shade trees. This was a revelation from the heavens. No longer would I be scolded for not closing the door because I was in a hurry. No longer would I dribble down the hall to the bathroom. No longer would I have to quit being Davy Crockett and go in the house. I could be Davy Crockett peeing in the woods.

Growing up in my family the thing that bound us together more than anything else was music. Music was sacred. We sang in church on Sunday and that brought comfort, but the music on summer nights brought joy. Fireflies came out at sunset like magic and lit up our backyard. Daddy and his friends were playing music on the back porch and the lightning bugs were the lightshow. The music, the laughter, homemade ice cream, and a Mason jar full of glowing bugs meant that all was right with the world.

The circle of wood, wire, and voices on our back porch that filled the air on any Saturday night worth remembering, shaped and molded me from a boy to a man. It taught me empathy, faith, profanity, manners, a love of brown whiskey, and the chords to "Long Black Veil." If I close my eyes on my own back porch strumming a beat-up Gibson flat top, I am instantly there again, standing on my mama's toes to dance with her before falling asleep to guitars, mandolins, and voices in harmony. A handful of years later my father would help me put my fingers on the frets. After awhile, I was allowed to join the circle on that porch with my own guitar.

Holy rituals are not always fun. If getting to stay up and listen to the music on Saturday nights was the high point, Friday morning Bridge Club was the low. It required model behavior and hygiene, neither of which came naturally to me. When it was my mother's turn to host, there was no Captain Kangaroo for me. Everything in the house had to be perfect. So, if Granny was not busy I could stay with her. She was not near as concerned about my hygiene. Oh, how I prayed she was not busy.

Granny lived in a small house at the far end of our backyard. I loved her fiercely. She never made me take a nap, always knew what was fun to play, and had invented mint Oreos by putting sticks of Wrigley's Doublemint gum in the cookie jar for a day. She was a genius.

She had a little flower garden in front of her house. On the Bridge Club morning most vivid in my mind, I asked her permission to water the window box and garden, knowing she might then let me play in the dirt. It was a warm day, even though it was late in the fall. I first had to water the black-eyed susans and hurricane lilies the way she had shown me, but after that I could make a mud mess by the fence and look for roly-poly bugs.

That morning just before lunch, all the ladies came outside to smoke, chat, drink coffee, and enjoy the sunshine. Normally I would not have even noticed them, especially since I had a pie pan full of roly-polies to play with, but I spotted the beautiful Mrs. Julia Ann Bell. She was younger and prettier than the other ladies, at least to me. She was slimmer but somehow curvier than my mother's other friends. I did not know why I always wanted to stare at her or talk to her, but I could not help myself.

I was mesmerized.

I stopped playing with the bugs and stood up, watching her laugh at something Mrs. Crosby was saying. I washed my hands in the hose and walked my muddy toes across the backyard toward them. My mother saw me coming and said, "Hey pumpkin, are you having fun at Granny's?"

"Yes, ma'am. Can I show Mrs. Bell all my roly-poly bugs?"

"Well, sure sweetie, if she's interested ... but now don't be disappointed if she is too busy talking to our other guests."

"Yes, Mama."

I walked over to the beautiful Mrs. Bell. Mrs. Sullivan was

talking and puffing a cigarette back and forth with the speed of a sports announcer, giving the play by play of her recent encounter with Lady Bird Johnson. Knowing not to interrupt, I stood, waiting my turn. Hearing a pause, like my mother said I should when waiting to speak to adults, I blurted out, "Y'all want to see my roly-poly bugs?"

"Well hey there, darlin'," said the beautiful Mrs. Bell, "Aren't you a sight. I bet this is your last barefoot day this year. You are lucky to have it so late in November. Mrs. Sullivan and I will both come look at them in a bit … as soon as she finishes telling me about Mrs. Johnson."

I waited as patiently as I could and rocked back and forth from one foot to the other while Mrs. Sullivan talked and talked. I started to make a little dance of my rocking and was mostly trying to catch the beautiful Mrs. Bell's eye. The moment I did, she gave me a little wink, held up a finger to Mrs. Sullivan, and giggled, "Come on, Angela, let's go see the boy's bugs."

That wink and giggle excited me so much that I was instantly hit with the need to go. I would never make it to the house. I would never last until I was down the hall or get the door closed and get my britches open without an accident. My muddy feet on Bridge Club day meant even further disaster. My salvation lay a mere ten steps away at the big pecan. I ran as fast as I could to the tree, as the two ladies set their coffee cups and saucers down on the patio furniture.

The moment I had the fly of my jeans open and aimed at the tree, Julia Bell put her hand on my shoulder and asked if this was where my bugs were. And I turned.

First relief then horror overwhelmed me as I peed all over the beautiful Mrs. Bell's black suede flats. She jumped back, Mrs. Sullivan shrieked, I turned toward her splattering the front of her gray herringbone pencil skirt. A chain reaction had begun. Six other women hearing Mrs. Sullivan's cry ran toward us, fearing some catastrophic injury. I panicked in response to the stampede and began running in circles, spraying anything or anyone in my path. Coffee cups, saucers, and cigarettes flew from their hands in their attempt to flee. I left none of the ladies unscathed. I had peed all over Bridge Club.

My bladder empty, my pants still unzipped, I fell in a heap on the grass, crying. My mother kneeled down, stood me up, and helped me get my britches back up and buttoned. She hugged, shushed, and consoled me until I stopped crying, not caring how dirty she got.

Granny saw the entire calamity from her front porch and as long as she lived, could tell the story better than anyone. As the Bridge Club ladies began to disperse (some teary-eyed from anger, others from laughter), she walked halfway across the yard covering her mouth with her hand, chuckling. She told my mother that she suddenly remembered she had a meeting down at the church. Then stifling a laugh, said, "Evelyn, this too shall pass." Mama shook her head, smiled, and handed me a bar of soap she kept on the back porch rail.

She pointed to the spigot on the side of the house. "Wash up! I'm gonna get you some lunch to eat out here and then you are getting a bath."

Mama didn't scold me 'til the ladies were all gone but once they were, she told me in no uncertain terms that I was never allowed to use a tree in front of company again, no matter how badly I needed to go. She finished off her warning with the worst words any boy wants to hear, "Little man, you and I and your Daddy are gonna have a talk about this when he gets home." I assumed the "talk" would be aimed at me and feared a spanking but years later realized that my father had much more to fear from that conversation.

I was eating my lunch on the back steps when I heard my father's car throwing gravel up the drive. It was way too early for him to be home. When he got out of the car, his face wore a grimace I didn't understand. My heart sank. He strode toward me in his suit, with his tie flying over one shoulder. When he scooped me up, I began to cry for the second time that day.

"Evelyn, Evelyn!" he called as he burst through the back door and plopped me on the couch. My mother ran crying to him and he grabbed her in his arms. She buried her face in his chest. The sight of my mother sobbing, shoulders heaving, terrified me.

I began to holler, "I didn't mean to, Mama, I didn't mean to! Daddy, please don't spank me!" Both parents looked at me bewildered, not understanding that I thought my mother's turmoil was my fault. No boy wants to be responsible for his mama's tears.

Mama kneeled down and hugged me. Daddy put his hand on my head, slowly rubbing my hair and in his deep voice said, "Nobody's going to spank you, son." Mama said, "This isn't about your accident at Bridge Club, sweetie." She took a deep breath.

"They've shot the president."

The TV was on all the rest of the day and into the night. Daddy never went back to work. Granny brought my older sister home early from school. The phone rang a lot. Relatives who never paid for long distance called. Our neighbor, Judge Mason, came by. He and my father whispered things I couldn't make out but I remember hearing the word "war." The grown-ups all spoke quietly and acted solemnly the rest of the day. They shushed me and my sister when some important development came on the television.

The whole house was silent when the newsman wept as he told us that John Fitzgerald Kennedy was dead. My mother and grandmother shed silent tears off and on that afternoon. I didn't know what to do. It was my first brush with grief.

That night, neither my sister nor I could fall asleep. My father got out the guitar and stood in the hallway between our rooms playing "Amazing Grace," "Puff the Magic Dragon," and "You Are My Sunshine" until we finally drifted off. He repeated that ritual many more times throughout my childhood and I continued that tradition with my own children.

The gift of simple yet elegant songs on a guitar, passing from generation to generation, began long before November 22, 1963, but it was exactly what we needed that night. Music comforted us after both I, and the whole nation, lost our innocence.

Listen to "Greatest Show on Earth," from the album For You to See the Stars by Radney Foster.

It Ain't Done with Me

The hand off was made in front of God and everybody at the Carousel bar in the Monteleone hotel. Always hide things in plain sight.

It looked like bribery or drugs or both, but they were pros, trained. I know a dead drop when I see one, even sitting at a bar in New Orleans that spins around before you start drinking. You never let go of certain things, like the need to learn the room. It doesn't take long, only a few seconds, but I am never comfortable 'til I've completed the scan. I've been out of the business more than ten years but there are habits I doubt I'll ever shed. They kept me alive.

I hadn't been in that bar since the first time I came to the French Quarter but she wanted to meet there. Since I was just shy of thirty when I last saw her almost twenty-five years ago, I figured I should let her experience the place however she desired. It's a Nola tradition and was her first time here.

I don't have a lot of regrets. I've tried to live my life so that they were minimized. The problem is life has a tendency to throw situations at us for which there is no easy answer. You are damned if you do and damned if you don't. No river, tide, nor baptism will wash you clean enough. Claire was one of those.

There are silly things we call regrets. I regret not losing my virginity to Mary Ellen Sinclaire on the night of our senior prom. She was ready and I wasn't smart enough to figure it out. Sharing that intimate moment with her would have been much less awkward than the reality I lived through on my first time. Those kinds of regrets are the ones you laugh at with old friends over bourbon on a screen porch in the cool of the evening.

Real regrets haunt you at sunset when the light reminds you of a tenderness you can never get back. They pull you back to an instant where all your choices were bad while you are standing in silence on a redfish flat. They wake you from a dead sleep. I have all the tools in the world to center the mind, care for my soul, surrender past mistakes to God, and move on. Real regrets? They don't give a damn. I regret killing two of the people I had to kill. I regret not being there when my father died. I regret leaving Paris.

She wore a simple white cotton skirt with a large red poppy print, a light blue sleeveless blouse with the collar turned up. She was tall with pale skin and wavy brown hair. She was elegant, carrying herself like a dancer in a Degas painting. She owned the room the moment she entered it. I raised my hand and made a quick small wave. Her smile was so genuine. Every man and woman in the bar watched as she strode toward me. I reached out to shake hands but she wagged a finger no, stood on tiptoe to kiss first my left cheek, then my right, and then my left again.

"Bonsoir, Claire."

"I have a picture of you from twenty-five years ago. You were so handsome. You have not changed." She had only a slight French accent, the giveaway being the soft *sh* sound in "changed."

"You shouldn't lean so hard into a lie like that, Claire. But thanks for flattering an old man."

She laughed. "You have to start the conversation somewhere.

I've obviously changed a lot. That's why I emailed a picture."

"I would have recognized you. Your smile is the same. Anyway, you look exactly like your mother."

She ducked her head. The sorrow mingled with anger that flashed in her eyes when she looked up again frightened me more than any mission I'd been a part of when I was still in business. For the first time in a long time I really had something to lose. The next few minutes of conversation, the explanations, could either foster or kill any hope of a future between us. My daughter's love was at stake.

We justify separation from kin. At times, we need safety. Distance to protect our hearts or our sanity. Most often though, we make excuses to justify our own selfishness or fear of rejection. I was sure that the paths I'd taken in life were the best decisions for both Claire and myself until that very second.

"Maybe we should start with what all unimaginative men in a bar ask a beautiful woman. Can I buy you a drink?"

The laughter came back into her eyes. "You're funny. Yes, please. I want to try the drink they have here in New Orleans. The one with the strange name I always forget."

"A Sazerac?"

"Yes, that's the one."

We made the small talk strangers make about vacations in a new city, slowly circling through the present, unable to tackle the past. She had too much planned for the next few days here. Those plans and her excitement again reminded me of her mother. We sat at the bar until I could no longer stand the slow spin most folks thought was fun.

"Are you hungry?"

"Starved! That Sazerac thing is strong. I need some food."

"You like seafood?" She nodded. "Come on, I'll take you to one of my favorite places in the world. It's not fancy but it's great."

It takes courage to wade into the river of more than two decades of rejection. That was my own fault. I left. I convinced myself that Claire was better off without me. Death had clouded my judgment. It always does. We make decisions to avoid pain. They rarely turn out well. I left Claire to suffer through not knowing why for years. It was my worst sin. I did not expect forgiveness but I needed to wade into the waters murky from unanswered questions if I wanted a relationship after tonight.

We ate charbroiled and raw oysters then split a plate of crawfish étouffée at Felix's up around the corner on Iberville. While Claire had dozens of questions for me about New Orleans and articulated the history she'd researched, the places she wanted to see, we had exhausted the small talk. The problem before us was that we could not speak meaningfully about the present without traveling through the past. Claire pulled a stray wisp of hair behind her ear, took a sip of white wine, looked up at me, and asked, "Where did you meet Pauline?"

I, Enrique Quiñonez Walker, do solemnly swear that I will support and defend the Constitution of the United States against all enemies foreign and domestic; that I will bear true faith and allegiance to the same; and that I will obey the orders of the President of the United States and the orders of the officers appointed over me, according to regulations and the Uniform Code of Military Justice. So help me God. Semper Fi!

I was seven when Johnny Varga came home in his uniform from boot camp to visit his folks. They lived across the street from us in the little town of Sabinal, Texas. He played touch football with us on a sunny fall afternoon. It seems odd now that a uniform would shape the future I had serving my country, but it may have been the biggest factor in forming my career and life. Johnny looked every bit a man and every bit a Marine.

By age thirteen I had a Marine poster on my bedroom wall. Unlike most boys in the 1970s I signed up for my first hitch when I turned eighteen in April of my senior year. My parents were both college grads and worried about me not heading that way. They shouldn't have. No one was prouder than my folks the day I graduated from Annapolis.

Being Hispanic despite my Anglo last name and light skin in South Texas in 1979 meant barriers abounded except in a uniform. The Marines make deer hunters into snipers and I was no exception. I out-shot everyone in San Diego and then out-shot most everyone else. I became a scout sniper with the 26th MEU until the commanding officer looking through my file discovered Lance Corporal E. Q. Walker was completely bilingual and saw my SAT score. That led to lots of tests, a congressional appointment, three new languages, and an infatuation with the Cyrillic alphabet.

"I met your mother in a pizza place in Paris near the Sorbonne. Two American boys flirting with two French girls."

"When did you know you were in love with her? Were you in love with her? I'm sorry … I have so many questions."

"No need to apologize. Yes, I was in love with Pauline. When did I know I was in love with her? A million different times, but the first was between midnight and one in the morning that first night."

She sighed. "I love that."

"She threw a shoe at me."

"What?"

"That was when I knew. She was a little drunk and she threw her shoe at me."

Claire cackled 'til she couldn't breathe. I smiled and continued, "I had just told her I was a Marine. We had been speaking in French. She asked where I'd learned to speak so well and I told her the Naval Academy and she freaked out. She cocked her head and asked, 'Navy?' I said, 'Marines.' Your mom was a Socialist. She screamed 'Merde!' and stomped off ten steps, realized we were in front of her apartment, turned, threw her shoe at me, and shouted in English 'You can't be so handsome and so nice and be a fucking Marine.'"

Claire sat gobsmacked, then began to laugh again. "And this made you fall in love with her?"

"Hopelessly."

Being a spy is a full-time occupation. You are never off the clock. Only a handful of people know your job description. You go places for extended periods where you can't call home. Life will forevermore contain secrets. The thing they don't tell you when you sign up is those secrets, if you let them, will over time keep you from truly being intimate with the ones you love.

My transition from Marine to Company man was an odd one. Most military personnel who go to work there do so after they're out of the service. There are exceptions. Those exceptions involve actual operations instead of analysis. The CIA wanted my language, sniper, and survival skills. They are in the business of information, the truth, if you will, but they are also in the business of lies. They never told me the truth about what my profession would cost.

"Were you there when I was born? I don't really know anything. I just have the one picture of you and my mother."

"Yes, it was the best day of my life. I fell in love twice that day. I fell in love again with Pauline for being so strong and brave ... then I fell in love with you the moment I held you."

Her eyes were misty and showed no anger. "You are a romantic."

"That I am. Let's take a walk."

As I opened the door, we were assaulted by the cacophony of Bourbon Street. Claire raised her voice to be heard over the din, "Why did you leave, leave her ... us?" A couple passing on the street gave us a shocked look then ducked their heads and kept walking. The directness of her question startled us all.

I could never properly answer that question, not to any satisfaction, neither for her nor me. The number of lost opportunities for me to have done something right, to change my relationship to Claire, were strewn over all those years like so many plastic hurricane cups in the gutter on Bourbon.

"Turn left, it's quieter that direction." It was easier for me to check for a tail on Royal than on Bourbon with its crowd of drunks, crazies, and gawkers. I felt the need to limit variables.

"Is that what your grandparents told you? When you were little?"

"They told me Maman had died. They said no one knew where you were. I was a persistent little *minion*. One day when I was nine, I kept after them wanting to know more. Papi was a little bit drunk and he stormed out the back door yelling that it was all your fault. He started to cry. I cried, too. Mami hugged me and told me not to listen to him. After that I knew not to push. When I was at university I did some research and found the records of the car accident that my mother ... I could find nothing about you that answered anything. It only made for more questions."

Strolling along Royal, I knew she was waiting for some answer that didn't have to do with abandonment, it had to do with death. I didn't have the answer she wanted. "It was all my fault. I let my job in service to my country get in the way of my family. It was a volunteer mission but as we say in the Marines, 'I was volunteered.' But truly I had a choice. I used to be an eternal optimist in addition to being a romantic. Your mama's death changed all that."

"According to the Marines, you are dead. Killed in '06 in Afghanistan."

"That's my story and I'm stickin' to it."

She laughed. We walked a half a block and I struggled with the best way to answer this and the series of questions I knew were coming.

"Yes, officially I am a dead Marine. Unofficially they still pay me, albeit through several cutouts. In actuality, I worked for the CIA after the first eight years of my military career. I was a spy when I met your mom. Well, not a spy yet ... just finishing my training. I didn't work in France per se. I was supposed to be a young businessman who traveled a lot. Your mother had her doubts ... but we were in love. We couldn't help ourselves. That's how we had you."

"Where were you when my mother was killed in the car accident? She was the only one in the car. How could it be your fault?"

"I was in Bosnia ... unable to communicate for long stretches of time, unable to tell your mother much. I couldn't tell your grandparents anything at all. It's why your grandfather, Étienne, blames me for her death. It's complicated and still hard for me to talk about. I didn't learn she'd died for four months. I was undercover ... deep."

I came home to Paris after ten bloody months in the field watching a country unravel. Bosnia was a beautiful place turned to hell itself by stupidity, hatred, fundamentalist nationalism, inability to compromise, lust for power, weapons, and the Cyrillic versus the Roman alphabet. Muslim versus Christian. Srebrinca killed any faith I had in my fellow man.

My sweet, sweet Pauline was dead. There were no loving arms to greet me, only the bitterness of Pauline's grieving parents holding a toddler's hand. Anger and the fear of me taking Claire from them fueled lawsuits. My covenant with the United States of America would not allow me to explain to Étienne and Anne Marie what I was doing and where I was those ten months. Pauline knew but could not explain from the grave. Eventually, Claire's grandparents and the French court system let me know I would no longer be able to see my three-year-old. Telling Claire now would make her question the love of her grandparents, the only parents she'd ever known. I could not do that to my daughter.

"I'm sorry for your loss of Étienne. What has it been? Five years now? I always knew when I couldn't be there, he would protect you. I would have written my condolences to your grand-mother … but I was afraid to risk it."

She looked down. "You know a lot. I miss him all the time."

"Let's walk two blocks up that way to Cosimo's. It's a dive bar but a good one. Plus it's quiet." I didn't want to tell Claire I was beginning to feel exposed. And I still had more to learn.

Charlene, the pretty brunette bartender with one crooked tooth in her smile and the blooming wisteria vine tattoo, read the fact that I was with a stranger the moment we walked in. No one realized she'd done it. She's good at her craft. She doesn't look like a federal case worker for those hiding in plain sight. That is the point. I turned to Claire, "Qu'est-ce que tu aimes?"

"Vin rouge."

"Charlene, the usual and a red wine for the lady."

The usual was Woodford's neat but it was also the signal that I was safe. We found a two top in the back.

"You went to elementary school at École St. Joseph and middle school at Cóllege Rosa Parks both in Les Andelys. High school you boarded during the week in Rouen … came home on weekends. You did very well on the Bac and went to the Sorbonne and a year of graduate school at Cambridge. You studied math, design, and of course English. I'd lost track after that … but I know you live in Paris."

Claire stared at me, mouth open. She couldn't hide her seething. Unlike her mother she didn't explode at me. Charlene brought the drinks and I smiled, thanked her. Claire didn't move or break her stare. Her long silence was heart-wrenching. She started slowly but the train gathered speed as her anger grew. "All those years, you made me wonder; I stared at that picture of you and Mamon. I dreamed about having a father. I pretended you would come driving up to our house to pick me up and take me to fantastic places all over the world. I prayed for you. All that time … you, you knew where I was and didn't care enough to find your own daughter. You piece of shit!" She was shaking.

She scowled in silence. I knew she wasn't finished and my speaking would not help matters. "Finding you was a fucking waste of my time." She started to get up.

"I saw you once when you were seven. You were playing in the schoolyard with the other little girls." She stopped. Sat back down, shaking again, and started to cry. I handed her my hand-kerchief. "You were so beautiful. I almost went to visit you at your grandparents that evening but it was too dangerous. I sent money for your care the entire time you were growing up. I know that's not enough though, really. I told you I was in Bosnia when your mother died. I had to go back there again. By the time I got back that second time you were well settled with Étienne and Anne Marie. Normally with a wife and a child I would have soon moved over to the analysis side or handled other operatives in the field. Your mama's death broke something in me. I was terrified to come and go from your life. The thought that I'd never be able to tell you where daddy was going or how long I'd be gone … and that every time I left I might not be coming back … well, it was more than I could handle. It's the biggest mistake I made in my life … not being a part of your life. It's my greatest regret. God, I hope you can forgive me."

I reached in my pocket and pulled out my money clip with cash, a license, a few credit cards, and a small laminated picture. In the photo was a little dark-haired girl in a red and white dress, church clothes. Her hands, feet, and face were a muddy mess. She wore a huge sheepish grin. I slid the picture across the table to Claire. "Your mom was mad as hell. We were supposed to be headed to your cousin's First Communion. You were too cute to punish. We both started laughing. It only encouraged your bad behavior." Claire laughed, put the picture to her chest, and started crying again. I conquered my fears and reached my hand across to hold Claire's. We both cried.

I spent my career serving my country in ways where no one sees your medals for valor and while there are rules, you are valued for your ability to color outside the lines. The Company sent me to some of the nastiest spots on earth for a decade and a half. In the Middle East, South America, not to mention the Horn of Africa, there are vast lawless terroritories that are complete clusterfucks. You can get killed there a half a dozen ways, on a good day. Russia's surrogates who like to curry favor with Moscow and in particular Vladimir Putin, play deadly games with us all the time. I'd served my country in places where power, greed, ideology, or all of the above had turned life for regular folks to hell itself. Where chaos was the norm and human life was of little value. I left a piece of my soul in them all.

It is not unusual to retire as a spy. It is not unusual for your career to weave back and forth between covert civil action and covert military action. What is unusual is the need to change your name, identity, and social security number. I killed only a handful of people in my career. Unfortunately, those kills were legendary in the intelligence and military community. I was outed. Whether by fame, infamy, or bad luck I have no idea, but there are those out there in the world who wish me ill. They live in the shadows and lust for revenge. I was now retired in New Orleans so that my past would not overwhelm my future.

There was still one thing to settle. It had haunted me from the first email I had gotten from Claire. Her finding me was a bird's nest of fishing line that she and I had to unravel, but it was much more dangerous than she realized. Either that, or she knew how dangerous. Which if true, could mean only one thing. She was a spook like her old man.

"Claire, crying makes me hungry. Have you ever had sweet potato fries?" I walked to the bar and ordered the fries and another round from Charlene, who looked at me to see if I'd blink. I did not. I sat back down. Claire was smiling at the picture I carried.

"How did you find James Lee Richardson?"

She looked up, smiled, and asked, "You mean you?"

"Well, that is who I am these days."

"It wasn't easy but not really hard either. I work for Propel in Paris. We do security and risk analysis for lots of companies. I do risk assessments for French and German firms that conduct business in South America. I decided to look up your service record one night after work. I was wondering about your death. Something that was declassified through the Freedom of Information Act had mentioned you indirectly concerning a company operating in Venezuela. It didn't make sense because you were stationed at a forward operating base in Iraq at the time. I spent a couple hours a night researching for two months."

"Wow, you were motivated."

"It became obvious to me after a while that you weren't killed in Afghanistan. My hope had been to find out how you really died. The more I researched the more it didn't add up. It drove me even more that by some crazy miracle my father might be alive."

"I get it. The curious part is how you made the leap from Enrique Walker to James Lee Richardson."

"I work with an internet bounty hunter who tests security for systems we sell to companies. He got me as far as Richardson and New Orleans. Some through hacking, some FOIA. I did the rest by looking up males in their mid-fifties. I narrowed it down to less than ten. Started making calls. You had no number but I kept looking. I found the lumber company you used to work for. Called to ask if you were really fluent in Spanish ... that you'd made a job application and I was checking your resume. They said you were. I told... Wanda? The lady on the phone. I said you hadn't filled out the email section on your application. She said, 'Oh, James Lee hates email but he will answer.' Then I emailed you. I was so thrilled when you answered."

Claire looked so happy in that moment. She was so proud of herself and in many ways I was too. She had all the brains and tenacity any parent would want for a child. She was beautiful and willing to travel across an ocean to follow her heart. It also broke mine. As she told her story, I knew what she didn't know. She came to meet me thinking reconnecting to her father would change her world. That finding me would fill a longing she'd had since childhood. Meeting me would change her life forever in good ways, but it stirred a hornet's nest she knew nothing about.

"Charlene, can you put all this on my tab? Oh, and call us a cab."

"Put this on my tab" was the signal to get me to safety.

"Sure thing James Lee. Ain't you got Uber in your phone?"

"Nope."

A black Cadillac Escalade pulled up within seconds. The two guys playing pool calmly laid down their cues and walked toward us. The taller of the two took Claire's arm as she got up looking confused.

"Careful, son. That's my daughter you got your hands on."

"Yes sir."

"Claire, they're gonna help us get out of here safely."

She went white with fear.

"Claire, I'm not going to let anything bad happen to you. We do, however, have to go quickly and quietly with these gentlemen for me to make good on that promise."

As we sped away into the Quarter and onto I-10 the young man in the front passenger seat turned to me and said, "Major Walker, sir, it is an honor to meet you. Your service to our country is legendary within the community. I am agent Brandon Wilson and we are taking you both directly to a safe house in Mobile."

Claire shouted, "What is going on? You can't just take me to Mobile! Let me out of this car. This is crazy!"

"Claire!" I shouted at my daughter for the first time in my life. The car went quiet except for the hum of the road. I let out a breath. "Claire, there are bad people in this world who would like nothing more than to hurt me, if for no other reason than the pride in doing so. Most of them learned long ago that I don't give a damn about what they do to me. But if you can find me, then they can find me. And if they can find me … then they can now find you. They would do many evil things to you just to get at me."

"Mon Dieu," she whispered.

"I've been done with the spy business for almost ten years. But apparently …" I blew out another breath.

"It ain't done with me."

Listen to "It Ain't Done with Me," from the album
For You to See the Stars by Radney Foster.

Isabel

I woke up naked in a strange room next to a beautiful, petite brown-skinned woman whose name I was clueless to recall.

While that may be some men's fantasy, the overwhelming awkwardness of the situation was more than I could handle. I had no idea what the hell had or had not transpired the night before. For possibly the first time in my life, I had a crisis of conscience as she walked with all her hip swinging glory in panties and tank top to her kitchen.

She put a cup of black coffee on the nightstand next to my pounding head. "Good morning." Her wry smile said she knew I didn't remember her name or much of anything else from the night before. She paused, as if waiting to see what I was really made of. Was I going to squirm in my hangover while hunting for clues to the previous night's adventures or summon up some dignity? She was playing me like a fish on a line, and we both knew it.

Fly fishing is a silent, meditative art. The way a long ellipse of fly line rolls out just above the stream and gracefully settles with the right amount of slack in the tippet, so that a dry fly lands stealthily on the water and will pass naturally over a trout, is a thing of beauty to me. If you can fool the fish well enough to eat the fly and are patient enough to wait to set the hook, an explosion of water follows. If that trout is a large rainbow or brown in a place like the Madison River outside Yellowstone, you will know it by the breakneck speed of the line ripping through your fingers. A tango has begun where the fish leads and you follow over rocks and water, the reel hissing at you as line peels off, while she heads downstream. Adrenaline has your heart pounding and a big part of your job is to stay calm and focused enough on the fish's dance steps to coax the beautiful creature into a net without harming either of you.

The signing was uneventful. There were no tears, regrets, or reservations at the time. It was not until the morning after my divorce that I realized how much my life was out of control.

The day the divorce was finalized had started as mundane as any. I had recently made partner at Gardiner, Thompson and Wynn in Dallas and I merely walked the block and a half from my office to my wife's attorney's office, signed, got a sandwich, and headed back to my desk. Now I was in a stranger's apartment, trying to piece together memories of the night before.

"And, how much of an ass did I make of myself last night?" was the best I could muster.

"Well, you did make an ass of yourself … but in a way you were a charming ass," she said. "At first you were funny, witty actually. Then you started getting really drunk."

"No one is ever attractive that way."

"You had your moments. Especially when you started talking about how the laws of silence don't work and how you were sorry for fucking up Jennifer's life."

"Ah," I said. "That's a quote by Tennessee Williams from

Cat on a Hot Tin Roof. I think silence had a lot to do with my marriage falling apart. Jennifer is my ex-wife as of ..."

"Yesterday," she said, finishing my sentence. "Isabel, my name is Isabel."

She explained that she had taken my keys in the parking lot of the bar where we met and drove me to her apartment, being unable to get any coherent address from me. I had at least made it to her bathroom to throw up. Short of getting me in a shower and to bed not much else had happened.

"Your clothes were a mess and I didn't have the heart to have you sleep naked on the floor in your condition ... so, I just spooned you 'til you fell asleep." She took a sip of coffee.

"Besides, it felt good to lay next to a man even if you weren't acting very manly. I'm going to shower and dress. You can borrow this 'til it's your turn in the bathroom."

She handed me a silk robe that barely came to mid-thigh and wouldn't close across my chest. I looked ridiculous. She confirmed that when she came out of the bathroom covering her mouth to stifle her laugh, and said, "That's a good look for you. The bathroom is all yours. Your clothes should be dry soon in the stackable. Take your time."

She had released me as tenderly as I would have returned a rainbow trout to the water, caught on a fly rod in a Colorado stream.

My ex-wife Jennifer was a sweet souled Methodist girl from Luling, Texas, when we met my senior year at UT. She had grown up with parents who instilled in her the best of small town American values. Love your neighbor, do your best at everything you do, if you get knocked down, get back up. They worked to give her the love, security, and ambition that she needed to make it in life and taught her she could be anything she set her mind to. She proved them right, busting out of that small town on the driving force of brains, commitment, and hard work.

In many ways, she was everything I was not. She was a lot like my father, though. He grew up a dirt poor farm kid of uncommon intellect from Palestine, Texas, and had worked his ass off to get us where we were in life. I, in turn, was raised in privilege in the Hyde Park neighborhood of Dallas, complaining when I had to drive his hand-me-down Beemer to school.

We were rich but not old money rich. I think that growing up around kids with enough spending money to buy blow while their folks were busy jetting off had an effect on me. I envied and despised them at the same time. I wanted to make them eat every smug word they ever uttered, but I also yearned to be just like them.

Jennifer and I were married after my first year of law school just as she graduated from UT. Things were good between us through law school, but once I started practicing, I was hell bent on being the biggest rock star lawyer Texas ever saw. I guess that was the beginning of our downward spiral. I think in some way my drive was attractive to Jennifer, and that she kept up with my excesses because her own dreams were of a high-powered career and a family. Still, her love was no match for my narcissism.

I quickly became bored with the entire game and tried to fill the void with cocaine, expensive alcohol, tumultuous affairs, and the rush of closing deals. I became adept at lying to her and we both were experts at keeping up appearances for the sake of my career. When I came home early one night and found her in bed with someone else, I had my excuse to end the charade, but I had driven her to it. I never wanted to hurt anyone, particularly Jennifer. I just did it anyway.

Standing in Isabel's shower that morning, with what felt like a river of water pouring over my pounding hangover, I knew something had to change. I didn't know the number of rivers I would travel to get there.

After I had gotten dressed, I asked Isabel if I could buy her breakfast. "It's the least I can do."

"It certainly is," she laughed. "I know just the place."

She took me to a hole in the wall in Oak Cliff for breakfast tacos and more coffee. "The menudo here is good for a hangover," she told me as we opened the screen door. The thought of tripe soup sounded like the last thing I needed. I ordered two bean and cheese tacos instead. While we ate, she clued me in some more on the previous night.

"I was having a cocktail with Greg Stallings from your office when you came up exclaiming that you were a free man." I mulled that over for a second. "That's beginning to come back to me. Greg left after a while. How did we ..."

"Get to my apartment?" she finished. "Before he left, Greg told me you were wild but harmless. We ate at the bar and you drank more than your fair share of Woodford's. You tried to kiss me in the parking lot, but you were way too boozy for that to happen. When you fumbled for your car keys, it was obvious I couldn't let you drive home. You were a mess. I didn't want to call the cops because I thought you might be an Officer of the Court, and God forbid I make you lose your standing, much less get you disbarred. I knew what I was getting into when I put you in my car."

I looked out the window and said, "You took pity on me, basically," thinking she may have not only saved my career but my life.

"Pretty much," she replied, hiding a mouthful of chorizo and egg taco with her hand.

As she drove me back to my car in the parking lot of last night's bar, she told me her story. She was a Latina from Del Rio, on the border in West Texas, and was just finishing a year as a clerk for a federal judge. She had gone to Michigan for law school and was interested in social justice issues, literature, faith in all its forms, mountain biking, and environmental law.

She was thinking through several offers from firms as a litigator for environmental causes.

"So, what kind of law do you practice?" she asked.

"Wall Street stuff, mergers and acquisitions mostly." She looked over at me, smiled, and simply asked, "Why?"

The question stung me. I realized instantly that I didn't have an answer, so I defaulted to the smartass reply, "Why not?" She cocked her head to the side, as if to ask a question, but never said a word.

When we pulled up to my car, she pulled out her card, scribbled her cell number on the back, and said, "Call me if you figure out the answer to that question."

She drove off.

Within a month of my conversation with Isabel, my desire to practice Wall Street law was completely gone. I had given Jennifer almost everything in our settlement. I thought, *I'll just make more.* Now, I wanted out of my current world. I resigned from the firm with calm but mercurial intention. I was aware of what I was giving up, but Isabel's one-word question and my lack of an answer had haunted me so much that I no longer cared.

It drove everyone from young associates to senior partners bonkers that I was leaving. I had been a hot shot on a stellar career path. "What the hell are you doing?" became the most common question I heard. They couldn't fathom throwing away the wealth and stature I had built in Dallas. "Something more than what I'm doing now," was my standard answer. It made me feel freer every time I said it.

I remembered a book I'd seen called *100 Best Trout Streams in America* and decided that, for the next year, I would put a large dent in it, checking rivers off my bucket list. I had grown up fly fishing with my dad on vacations in Colorado and had fond memories of it. Those were the few times when I didn't feel agitated as a teenager. Something about the voice of the water and the rhythm of the cast were calming, like a song on a gut string guitar played soft and low. I needed that song.

I started by selling or donating everything I had left except for camping and fly fishing gear. I had just enough cash to live frugally for nine months or more if I had no rent or obligations. I made a vow to myself to fish for a year. I'd been pretty lousy at keeping vows, but this was one I thought I could honor.

I bought a used Ford F-150 with a camper top, rigged it with damn near as much fishing and fly tying materials as a well-stocked fly shop, and headed to Livingston, Montana.

It was amazing how quickly I transformed into a typical trout bum with no particular place to go and no schedule to keep. I was adrift, but I decided to lean into that wanderlust and I didn't care what anyone thought. I traded being one kind of bum for another.

The Gallatin, the Yellowstone, the Henry's Fork, the Snake, the Teton, and the Madison are rivers whose names are as revered in fly fishing as the books of the New Testament are to Christians. I fished them all, working my way south.

It was the best wasted time of my life. I read Henry David Thoreau, Mark Twain, John Muir, Jack Kerouac, John Steinbeck, and Cormac McCarthy; not because someone told me to but just for the sheer pleasure.

The card Isabel gave me lived in the plastic sealable wallet where I kept my fishing licenses. Every time I bought a license in a new state, there it was. I'd take it out and roll it over a few times, think about calling her, and put it back. I wasn't ready. Her card was a nagging reminder of my inability to dig through the mess I had made of my life, but I couldn't toss the little rectangle.

"Oh shit! That's a good fish!" There was no one but prong horned antelope on the hill to hear me. After a fight through 40 yards of fast water and a banged up shin, I was able to gently pressure him into a soft back-eddy pool. I didn't bother to take a picture of that 20-inch brown trout. I had no one to share the memory

with of that late October day on the Firehole River. My memory would be enough.

As winter began to come on, I headed to the Gulf Coast of Texas and Louisiana. I bought a cheap johnboat, satisfying my flyrodder habit on redfish flats and bayous where no one else seemed to be paying attention. When the tides or the weather were uncooperative, I read all the books I wished I'd taken the time to read earlier in my life. My tastes in literature followed my southern path. Flannery O'Connor, William Faulkner, Toni Morrison, James Lee Burke, and Tennessee Williams kept me company.

As spring began to come back to life, I sold the boat and bought a kayak intending to head north and fish my way back to Yellowstone followed by Idaho, Oregon, and Washington. Before that though, I had a smallmouth bass destination on the wilds of the Devil's River in Texas that I wanted to check off my list.

When I hit Del Rio, Texas, I made the hard right on US 90 to head north to the Devil's and pulled into the first gas station I saw. The pumps looked like a movie set from the 1960s. As I headed inside to pay, I walked directly into a woman with brown hair and dark eyes, in a silk charcoal silver dress. She blew past me with an "Excuse me."

"Isabel Villareal?" She turned and looked at me confused, not recognizing me at all. I realized I had not shaved or cut my hair since beginning my pilgrimage, nearly nine months ago.

"David Caldwell, we spent an evening together several months back that you would probably prefer to forget. I owe you an apology."

"You came all the way from Dallas to apologize?" She laughed, but didn't look particularly amused.

"No, no," I sputtered, trying to unravel the mental spaghetti between us. "I'm headed to fish the Devil's River. I've run into you by accident. Sorry about my appearance. I'm not currently practicing law and I've barely spoken to a soul in the last several months. I've been on sort of a journey of rediscovery." I realized I was babbling, slowed down, and said, "You look stunning. You must be headed to a party."

"Yes," she said, already starting to back toward her car. "My sister is getting married tomorrow. I'm actually headed to the rehearsal dinner right now. It's nice to run into you. Good luck with the, uh, fishing." With that, the woman who had inspired this sojourn with a single word sped off into traffic.

I looked around. I had been on the road for ten hours and was bone tired. Another night sleeping in my truck in some Walmart parking lot was more of a pain in the ass than I wanted to endure. Plus, even though it was only May, it was nearly 100 degrees.

I splurged on a cheap motel room, looked in a mirror for the first time in months, and realized why Isabel had reacted the way she did to my new look. *David, you might want to rejoin civilization a little bit.* I bought a razor and shaved. I walked into a Quick Cuts up the street and told the woman with an empty chair that I needed a haircut.

"No kidding, sweetie," she drawled.

As she snipped away my wild man hair, I asked where to find the best Mexican food. She told me to skip the places on the highway, and instead go all the way into town, to Memo's, where the food was great and the band could play anything from Latin Jazz to Western Swing. I showered, ironed a shirt for the first time since leaving Dallas, and headed out.

As I pulled up to the restaurant, I could hear vibes and sax wailing on Tito Puente's "Oye Como Va." *Man, she wasn't kidding about the band.* The place sat on a fantastic spring-fed creek where a family was having a picnic on the far bank. The fisherman in me couldn't resist a look at the water before going in to eat. After watching a few pan fish work the edges, I turned and saw Isabel through the plate glass window, seated at what was obviously a long table set especially for the wedding party. I stared at her. I couldn't help myself.

I was just about to leave, knowing that staying was probably a bad idea, when she turned to look out the window, taking a sip from a margarita. Rage filled her face as she slammed down her glass. I mouthed the words, "Oh shit."

The next thing I knew, she stormed through the exit door spewing hellfire and Spanish. "What the fuck are you doing?" ripped through the air loud enough to startle the family on the opposite bank. "Why are you following me? How did you know I would be in Del Rio? Is this some kind of a sick joke? You are creeping me out, first with your crazed homeless guy disguise and now following me here. I'm not letting you ruin my sister's wedding!"

I kept backing up, trying to explain, until I was up against the creek bank. She shoved my chest with a "leave me the hell alone" gesture. It was just enough to tip the balance in favor of the creek.

When I emerged sputtering from the water, the wedding party and other curious onlookers were on the bank laughing. Isabel spun on her heel and stomped away. As I climbed out of the water, a beautiful middle-aged woman who was obviously Isabel's mother laughed and said, "I hope you'll forgive my daughter's temper. You two must be … friends?"

"Ma'am, this is truly my fault. I think the coincidence of me being here took Isabel by surprise. Congratulations to you and your family on your daughter's wedding." I turned, made the wet walk of shame to my truck, with laughter, conversation, and Mrs. Villareal calling "Come back!" trailing behind me.

I woke up early the next day bemused by the combination of humiliation and lust swimming through my brain. I couldn't help but laugh out loud. *Head upstream, buddy.*

The limestone bottomed Devil's River weaves its way through untouched country in the deserts of West Texas. As you float down, you can spy 12,000-year-old pictographs in the cliffs above. Cholla, prickly pear, lecheguilla, and sagebrush along the shore make a beautiful green, gray, and slate backdrop to the emerald and aqua swirling pools and riffles. The fact that the Devil's River is also filled with trophy smallmouth makes it a perfect fly fishing dream.

The hauntingly stark landscape, so pristine, desolate, and unpeopled, was a metaphor for my journey of the last several months.

Lying in a tent after the two-day float, I was kept awake as nature, a gorgeous angry woman, and a search for purpose all wrestled in my mind.

I drove north the next day to New Mexico, trying to figure out how to resolve a comical but real conflict with a woman I barely knew, but would like to know. Walking out of a Best Buy with a newly activated iPhone, I dug through my bag and found her card. It sat beside me on the seat for the next sixty miles. *Screw it, you have nothing to lose.* I dialed the number.

"Hello?" I was prepared to leave a message and startled when she answered. "Uh … Hello, Isabel, it's David Caldwell and I wanted to apolo …"

She cut me short. "No, no, no, I owe you a big apology. I realize it really was coincidental that we ran into each other. Plus, my mother talked me out of my tree."

"Your mother is delightful and beautiful. Listen, I won't bother you again, but I did want to tell you that your 'why?' in the parking lot in Dallas has haunted me, helped me make some big changes. I ended up quitting GT&W, rethinking my life and what I ought to do with it. I suppose, I really just wanted … to thank you."

Her two-second pause felt like an hour. "Wow, I drove off that morning thinking 'Isabel, why did you act so bitchy and smug with him?'"

"Well, it worked," I laughed. "I've been fly fishing, reading, and pretty much being a hermit trying to figure out my life for nine months."

"Amazing. It's cool that you've been afforded that time and

space. Not very many of us get that luxury." She paused. "I'm sorry, I hope that didn't come off badly. I'm from a working-class family and proud of it. To be able to do that sounds glorious … but for me … impossible."

"No, no," I replied, seeing the perspective of someone who didn't come from money for perhaps the first time. *Damn, every time I talk to this girl it gets down to the bones of the matter.* "Thank you for being honest. I made a lot of money and most of it went to Jennifer in my divorce, but I had enough left over to be able to spend a year in this camper rethinking things. I'm going to need a job soon. I'm just not sure I'm ready to practice law again … at least not the kind of law I was practicing before. There's not anything wrong with it. It's just not for me."

There was a long stretch of silence and then she asked what I'd been reading. I waxed on and on about Thoreau, Hemingway, and Steinbeck before she interrupted and said, "You know my father always said there are three sides to everything. The physical, intellectual, and spiritual. It sounds better in Spanish, 'carnal, mental, y espiritual.' I keep listening about your escape from the world, but I'm not hearing anything about any spiritual journey."

Why the hell are conversations with this girl so intense? "You've got a point," I said lamely.

"Ever read Thomas Merton?"

"Who?"

"Thomas Merton, he was a Catholic monk and a mystic. He wrote about all the things you are talking about. You should check out *Mystics and Zen Masters.* It was one of my favorites in college."

"Wow, yeah, I'll do that." We talked on for over an hour about everything from literature, low riders, oil drilling, art, and feminism to quinceañeras. Finally I said I needed to drive on and find a camping spot before dark.

I fished the San Juan River the next two days, rolling my conversation with Isabel through my mind the entire time. Sitting with a bourbon by my campfire that second night, I decided to search for a bookstore the next day.

I hit the jackpot in Durango, Colorado—a crazy used bookstore in an old house that was stacked floor to ceiling with books in no apparent order. Yet the owner knew where every book was, magically leading you through the maze of rooms and makeshift shelves to find what you wanted. Stacked on top of Julia Child's *The Art of French Cooking* was *Mystics and Zen Masters*, and another Merton title *Thoughts in Solitude*. I bought them both.

That night, I started my card flipping ritual again. *Ah, what the hell. Who says it's too soon to call?* I dialed Isabel. I told her Merton was so different than anything else I'd read. "I'm not sure what to do with it." I made her laugh with my description of the nutty bookstore. She described growing up Roman Catholic in a Mexican American culture but challenging everything. "My freshman year of college I was queen of the radical rejecters. No shaved legs for me."

We talked for almost two hours.

I intended to fish the Animas but I took a side trip to Mesa Verde National Park to see the cliff dwellings. Over a thousand years ago, the Pueblo tribes built elaborate stone "apartment" villages in the cliff overhangs and caves beneath the mesas of southwest Colorado. After living there almost three hundred years, they completely abandoned them. No one really knows why. I wanted to see it for myself.

The cliff dwellings are beautiful and fascinating. Watching the sunset turn them gold, red, and purple took my breath away. I thought I would only spend a couple days there but something about the mystery and beauty of those ruins held me for almost a week. I spent my days on guided tours, climbing through the ruins, and on quiet hikes by myself. I stayed up nights devouring Merton.

I had rarely if ever thought about God and wasn't sure he, she, or it existed. My parents hadn't been very religious, and

I had only a handful of recollections of ever being in church. I owned no Bible, Koran, Baghava Ghita, or any other sacred books. That night, while lying in the bunk of my camper and mulling over the beauty of the Mesa Verde sunset, the beguilingly smart and sexy Isabel, and the writings of a monk I'd hadn't heard of a week before, I prayed my first prayer: "I don't understand You."

A campsite near Durango was my headquarters for the next week, but the fishing was terrible. Tangled lines, lousy drifts, and high water led me to put up the rod and spend my time reading and eating green chile cheeseburgers most days. I went back to the crazy bookstore where, once again, the guy behind the counter knew where to find everything, despite the apparent chaos.

"There are two modern English translations of the Bible on the green wall, two rooms down underneath a stack of Ray Bradbury."

I bought my first Bible and thumbed through as I headed to the truck. The first thing I read was, "Woe to you lawyers! For you have taken away the key of knowledge."

"Shit!" I tossed the book in the passenger seat. "This is about to get weird."

I thought Isabel would get a kick out of my Bible story, and sure enough, she cracked up. "Yeah, Jesus doesn't have a lot of good things to say about us lawyers."

"Well, apparently I quit the law just in time. You on the other hand ..."

She roared with laughter. "You can be a Christian and a lawyer. You just have to work a little harder. In court I'm called Counselor and my faith makes me want to live up to that name. I want to help others and my best shot at that is to give them wise counsel."

My silence must have betrayed how dumbstruck I was.

"I was born to a Catholic family," she said, "but faith isn't really inherited. For a while I thought I was an atheist but that didn't work for me anymore. My faith isn't my parent's, it isn't the Church's, but it is faith. It works for me."

"How did that happen?"

"It was a winding path but in a nutshell, an Episcopal family in Del Rio, a very cool nun, and a lesbian fling in college."

"Walk into a bar?" I joked to hide my panic.

She chuckled. "You made me spew my tea. You're still funny. I'll tell you the whole story the next time I see you … college adventures and all … but you have to promise not to get a chubby," she joked.

"I can make no promises concerning that part of my anatomy. It has a mind of its own."

She laughed again. "Spoken like a true attorney. Look, start with the Gospels: Matthew, Mark, Luke, and John. Read Luke first; it has the Christmas story. Then read John, the brainiac's gospel, and then the other two."

She said she had finally moved to Denver to work for an environmental firm and was settling in. As she hung up all I could think of was, *"the next time I see you." She wants to see me again.*

The mountain runoff in the Rockies makes most of the rivers unfishable in late spring, with the exception of some remarkable tailwaters below dams, so I headed to the Taylor River near Gunnison. The catch and release section below that dam is filled with obscenely large trout that are extremely wary. Catching a trophy fish there is an accomplishment. I fished early in the morning and late in the afternoon to avoid the crowd of other anglers. During the middle of the day, I read the Bible, Merton, and John Gierach's essays on fly fishing. The cell reception was terrible. I kept finding myself driving toward Crested Butte 'til I got reception to call Isabel.

I hooked up on a 27-inch monster rainbow at sunset on my fourth evening there. It was really too heavy to land by myself and the only other people around were a family on the bridge downstream. The dad asked if I needed help landing that huge fish and I took him up on it. He took a few pictures of me holding that beauty and his whole family marveled as I gently released her to the water and watched her glide away. He said, "That's a once in a lifetime fish. I'm glad God gave us the chance to see it."

We shook hands, my chest still pounding with adrenaline. I said, "Wow, thank you, too cool, enjoy your evening."

He turned and walked away up the path, put his arm around his wife, and held his daughter's hand. In that instant, the joy of that once in a lifetime fish meant nothing. I left the water, packed camp, and drove all night, determined to make Denver.

I got a couple hours of sleep in the parking lot of a grocery store in Golden. About eight the next morning, I bought a cup of coffee and texted Isabel, "You up?" She called right back. I asked if I could buy her dinner and told her I had been reading and was filled with questions.

"Sure, are you coming to Denver soon?"

"I'm here now in the parking lot of … uh, King Super. Could I take you out, tonight?"

"Wow, uh … yes. It's only my second week at my new firm, and I'll have to move something around, but yes."

"Let me take you someplace nice, you pick. Text me where and when."

"I will, I've got to get back to work now. We'll talk later."

"Shit, that's right, you're a lawyer." She laughed at that and hung up.

I spent the day re-entering the world of a city. I found a mall, walked into Nordstrom's, and bought a blazer and a western pearl snap dress shirt. I got a hotel room and cleaned up. By the time I stepped out of the cab at the Italian restaurant in pressed Wrangler jeans, polished Luchesse boots, and new shirt and jacket, no one would have guessed I had been living in a camper for ten months. I ordered a glass of wine and some olives at the bar while I waited.

Isabel walked straight up to me and kissed my cheek. "You clean up good."

"Don't let it fool you, I'm still living in my truck." She was wearing a blue cocktail dress and heels and looked stunning.

Dinner was delicious but that is all I remember about the food. I was completely destroyed by the beauty and intelligence of the woman across the table. She talked about her life with unblushing honesty and complete lack of pretense. She told me about growing up on the Texas border, working her way through college, and receiving a Darrow Scholarship to law school at Michigan. Her stories were woven together as if they were parables. We talked about faith, poetry, literature, and the law. I had never in my life asked myself the kinds of questions she asked.

We wore out our welcome after three hours at the dinner table so we left and walked through the cool almost summer evening. "I'm still searching for a good answer to your original question when I was hung over that morning in Dallas. In some ways I hope I never find it, 'cause … I'm different because of it."

"How?"

"I've always been a numbers and logic kind of guy. I like things cut and dry … the law. You look at life and it's blurry … but you're good with that. You ask me questions that have so many different angles but never say any of my answers are wrong."

"Well, actually … most of your answers are way off base," she teased, "but it wouldn't be right for me to tell you 'you're wrong.' Seriously … it's not my job. I know the right answer for me but my path isn't yours. Jesus told us to love one another how we wish to be loved. Pretty simple, right?"

"Well, kind of. I'm not that sort of guy. I like solid answers."

"Ahhh, you want God to be an equation. God is a poem."

That floored me.

It was getting late when we walked back toward the restaurant. At the corner I leaned down and kissed her. We stood there kissing a long time and I'm sure people stared but we didn't care. As she gave me a ride back to my hotel, our conversation came to a standstill. Anticipation of the possibility of naked intimacy with her took over all the spaces in my brain. In the portico of the hotel, I asked her to stay with me and she said she couldn't.

"Am I being too forward?" I asked.

"Oh no, I want to fuck your brains out, but there's a problem."

"Whoa! OK ... I wasn't expecting that answer," I laughed. "I guess the next question is what's the problem? Is it a Catholic, uh ... Christian thing?"

"No ... and yes ... the problem is my heart's involved and if I go up to your room, I'm not just going to have sex with you, I'm going to make love to you. My heart and soul will get all tangled up and I'll get my heart broken."

"What if I said I'm falling in love with you?"

"You'd be lying. If you were falling, you would just say it."

"OK, I'm a little stung by that statement because I'm definitely falling. Is there a way to cleverly lawyer my way out of this mess and you still come upstairs?"

"There you go making me laugh again." She smiled and kissed me. "I'm going to drive away now before I change my mind."

I called her the next morning. We talked for an hour and there was no awkwardness in her voice. I asked if seeing her again tonight was too soon and she said no, but that she was going to Mass at 5 o'clock.

"On Saturday?"

"There's a lot of us Catholics. So we have times for Mass all weekend."

"Why don't I come with you and then take you to dinner?"

"OK, but this Mass is in Spanish. You might not understand it."

"Perfect," I laughed. She said to come twenty minutes early to her new place and we'd walk to church and she'd make dinner after. "It'll be my first dinner in my new house."

After I hung up, I drove an hour out of town to Deckers, Colorado, to fish on the South Platte River. *I should bring Isabel up here. It's beautiful.* For two hours, in the soft seams next to the bank, I nymphed a bead head pheasant tail and a tiny midge fly that I'd tied. I was rewarded with at least eight trout. One of which was close to twenty inches and had some of the most brilliantly colored spots I'd seen on a brown. I took a picture to show Isabel. The fishing was on fire and I would normally have stayed 'til dark, but I gently reunited that fish to her home and headed to Denver.

If you're leaving water this good to go to church with a girl, you're in trouble, brother.

I pulled up in front of a 1930s bungalow and Isabel came to the door in a lavender print dress with a black lace shawl over her shoulders. Her beauty left me speechless. We walked to church like a couple of teenagers dawdling, thinking about cutting class. The service had already started when we walked in. The hymn being sung with the pipe organ sounded familiar and I realized it was a classical piece I knew but couldn't put my finger on. The music and liturgy wove back and forth between things I understood and didn't, between modern and ancient, between Mariachi guitars and Bach interludes, like the oxbows of a trout stream in a meadow. Something mysterious in me wove back and forth with it. My lack of knowledge of Spanish allowed me to stop thinking, and let the beauty of the service transport me. My soul slid stealthily into that stream of faith and pageantry hoping to remain unnoticed, like any good fisherman.

As Isabel got up to take communion, she placed the thin translucent lace shawl on her head. Time stood still. Her beauty performing this centuries old ritual washed over me and tears washed my face.

When we got back home I walked in and was amazed. It was filled with books and framed photographs that she had taken all over the Southwestern United States and Northern Mexico intermingled with pieces of religious folk art from the same region.

She had a bottle of Rioja, two glasses, and a small clay pitcher filled with miniature white roses on her kitchen table. "Wow, this is beautiful ... and I just realized I'm showing up empty-handed. I should have brought you a hoursewarming gift." She leaned up on tiptoe, kissed me on the lips, and said, "That's OK, I'll let you figure out a way to make it up to me."

She opened the back door to a very small yard with a patio, garden, and cedar privacy fence. The door, post, and lintel had been decorated with all manner of folk art and iconography—miniature silver hands, feet, crosses, and hearts. They had been artfully nailed into the pattern of a cross in the center. After she lit the charcoal grill, Isabel lit a small stick of incense and put it in a folk art piece on one of the doorposts.

"It's beautiful," I said. "I've never seen the hearts with crowns and ... rays of light? I suppose they all mean something." She laughed. "Sure, they mean something ... but it is special to me because I made it as a prayer. The incense is really a prayer, too ... you know, like a candle at church. Although I don't have to pay extra when I light 'em here at home." She winked at me.

We moved her kitchen table outside and ate dinner under the stars. She talked about the church service, food, fly fishing, and the wine we were drinking. Her voice captured my heart the same way it did when we were on the phone. We finished dinner and lingered over the wine. All I wanted to do was take her in my arms but I held back. Instead, I got up and started clearing the table. She came up behind me and wrapped her arms around my waist as I washed the dishes. "Stop," she whispered. I turned around and kissed her for a long time. I wanted terribly to go further, but remembered the night before and what she had said about her fears of falling in love. Before I had time to think too much, she had unzipped and shimmied out of her dress.

"I thought you were worried I would break your heart and it wasn't worth the risk." She took a deep breath, leaned against my chest, and sighed. "I know but I can't stand it anymore so I'm jumping."

"It's not much of a risk ... I'm falling in love with you."

Clothes flew, kisses pressed, breathing swelled, and muscles flexed all over her kitchen, living room, and finally to her bed. That frenzy ended with the moans and cries of much more than good sex. She had thrown her soul and heart into the process. As we lay in each other's arms, I knew I would never be the same. We fell asleep.

I smelled coffee as I woke and felt the other side of the bed for Isabel. She wasn't there. I peeked one eye open and saw the clock by my head said 9:30. Isabel came in and put a cup of coffee on the nightstand six inches from my one open eye.

"You've developed a habit of bringing me coffee in the morning," I said sleepily, "I've woken up next to you twice and you've done it both times." She smiled and said, "The first time doesn't count. I was trying to get you out of my bed that morning."

I took a gulp of coffee and was quiet.

"You have more monkish wandering to do, don't you?" she asked as she stood over me with her hip against my shoulder.

"It's your fault," I said, "you introduced me to a monk named Merton. Although I'm not sure last night could be described as monkish in any way."

She hummed a small laugh. "That's not really what I meant. I know your searching isn't finished."

"I'm going to need a couple cups of coffee and a minute to give you a real thoughtful answer." *Last night changed things.* "Can I take you someplace for breakfast in a bit?"

"Yes, please," she said as she kissed my temple, walked to the bathroom, shed her robe without closing the door, and started the shower.

Over huevos rancheros and a bowl of posole, I finally was able make sense of my confusion. "Isabel, every time I talk to you, I tell you things ... and thoughts ... I don't tell anyone. There's a big part of me that wants to stop this crazy fishing, reading, whatever kind of journey I set out on and stay here with you … but I committed myself to a year and I need to honor that promise. I spent a long time not living up to any promises I made. I don't ever want to go back to that."

"I know. That's why I told you, you still have wandering to do. You should finish the commitment you made for yourself. I don't want you to go … but I won't let you stay either."

"You confuse me. Nothing lines up with you. You are this amazing swirling ball of contradictions. A feminist, evangelical Catholic … and a mystic who liberally disagrees with her own church. You love art and literature but you're a scientist at heart. You're a lawyer but don't act like one. You know Mexican and American history I've never heard of. You listen even when I rattle on about fly fishing. I'm addicted to you."

She sat in silence then winked at me and asked, "You done?" I nodded. She said, "A girl likes to stay mysterious. Keeps guys like you on your toes." She reached across the table and ran her hands down my arms. "Talking and listening to you on the phone is what has been making me fall in love with you, but your heart is searching … and I would be a fool to stop you. Don't take this wrong … but you'll never fully fall in love with me if you don't go away. You need that search or you'll regret it later. So go be Jacob and wrestle with the Angel."

"Huh? Who is Jacob?"

She laughed out loud. "Bible story. Come here, *vente*." She beckoned across the table and said, "Taste this," as she held out a big spoonful of posole that she had dressed with avocado, fresh jalapeño, radishes, and cilantro. I took the mouthful and closed my eyes as I was engulfed by spice and flavor. "That, Cariño, is the flavor of me. It is ancient and spiced with love and care and a culture that built pyramids. If you want that, you can wander wherever you need to, but you come back to me."

"Oh God, you are sexy."

"Yes, I am."

I laughed. "But I'm no closer to knowing the answer to that first question you asked me. That 'Why?' was a lot bigger than I thought."

"It was bigger than I thought. Now that I think about it … maybe it wasn't me asking. God uses us when we least expect it."

"So ten more weeks of fishing, reading, thinking, and … now maybe even praying?" We both laughed.

For the next couple of months I traveled to several rivers and streams that were on my list but always returned within a week or so to Isabel. We made love, talked for hours, and lost sleep. I learned to pray. Well really, I learned to talk to, cuss at, and listen to God. By the end of several weeks, something lodged inside my soul.

Thomas Merton said, "Only the man who has had to face despair is really convinced that he needs mercy. It is better to find God on the threshold of despair than to risk our lives in a complacency that has never felt the need of forgiveness."

I never knew I wanted forgiveness until I wanted Isabel. In the past, I just walked away from those I hurt or put up a wall to make them walk away from me. I didn't just want Isabel's love, I wanted to keep it, and that would require learning about forgiveness. Most nights while away, I called her. My chest ached at the pull of her as we talked late into the night. My last trip before landing a job at a fly shop in Denver was to the Madison River at Three Dollar Bridge just outside Yellowstone. I had promised myself I would fish 'til my thirty-fourth birthday. I caught a nice healthy male rainbow about 9:00 a.m. on that August 26th and thought, *This journey is over, it's time to start a new one.* I left the water and drove ten hours straight through to Denver.

It has been three years now since Isabel and I fell in love. When I left Yellowstone on the morning of my birthday, I swore I wouldn't come back to that amazing place without her. I wanted to share its beauty with her. It wasn't a hard sell. We've spent our last two vacations here, always around my birthday.

This year, we weren't floating the river. I made a picnic spot with a blanket and lots of pillows to try and make her swollen belly comfortable. I had told her we could skip the trip up here this year but she had insisted. "We came here on our honeymoon. I love this place," she said and kissed me as I rubbed her belly. "Besides this baby is coming late. Just ask my mother. Plus, you are gonna need this calm. You are about to live through the birth of a Villareal grandchild! Good luck, Cariño."

Listen to "Raining on Sunday," from the album
For You to See the Stars by Radney Foster.

Belmont and Sixth

When the light turns green the relationship is over.

I always pull away into traffic with a bitter cocktail of guilt, anger, sadness, and there-but-for-the-grace-of-God-go-I humility. I can usually shake it off by playing some music. There are times it lasts longer but eventually I let it go. That was true until yesterday, when I met Will. He changed the rules of the game and I'm not sure I can forgive him.

He was working the line of traffic at Belmont and Sixth, a few blocks from my office, holding up the latest edition of *The Shelter*. I'd bought a paper or two from him before so I could put it on the dash. That was my signal that we were solid 'til the next edition came out.

I would ask, "How ya doin'?" and he would answer, "Better all the time. Almost nine. Cars in line. Better all the time." He smiled and was funny but we steered clear of meaningful conversation. I felt better about myself and he made a buck or two.

Yesterday we both broke the rules. I spoke first but it's his damn fault. It was barely twenty degrees and the wind was howling. I noticed he was limping and had duct tape wrapped around his left shoe. "What happened to your foot?"

"Ah, bicycle accident, but you should see the other guy." He winked.

"How's the bike?"

"Pretty much toast. The light's green, buddy. Don't want to tax the patience of my customer base. Paper chase."

I laughed, handed him a five, and told him to keep the change. He waved as I rolled up the window. A minute later I was about to pull in to the parking lot at work. "Shit, I don't have time for this." *That guy wrecked the bike he uses to get from wherever he sleeps to that corner to sell those street papers. Now he's got a bum leg and his shoe is torn up.*

"Shit, shit, shit!" I pounded the steering wheel. *I do not have time for this.*

I pulled around the two blocks, got back in his lane of traffic, and waved him down. "You seen a doctor?"

"No way, Jose." He shook his head and looked at me as if I were stupid for asking.

"You're gonna need some new shoes as cold as it is; that left one's doing you no good. There's an Army/Navy surplus store a few blocks away up on Highland. Let me take you over there and get you a pair of boots."

"Sir, that's real nice and all," he cleared half the gravel from his throat and spat, "I mean no disrespect but I've gotta make my money for the day, now ... during rush hour."

"I never thought of that. How much you expect to make in the next hour?"

"Twenty bucks if I'm lucky. Nothing if I'm not." The rest of the gravel seemed permanent.

"I'm good for the twenty and the boots. Hop in the car ... ugh, I mean get in the car."

He laughed, "You're mighty kind. Mighty kind. Just let me get my backpack and papers." He limped to the corner as I rolled up slowly.

"Hey, you mind if we pull through that Bojangles so I could buy a chicken and biscuit … I mean, I mean, I won't eat it in here, I don't wanna mess up your car. I'll save it for later."

"I haven't had chicken and biscuits in ten years. It sounds delicious. I'm buying."

"You're a preacher aren't ya. You're too nice. Too nice. I knew it. What kind? I got a bed tonight in the gym at First Methodist 'cause it's so damn cold. I like them. They don't preach too hard at ya."

"I'm not a preacher. I'm Josh Bateman, I'm an account manager at … never mind, I crunch numbers for a living. What's your name?"

"Will."

"Well, Will, nice to meet you."

As I turned into the Bojangles, I said, "Let's just go inside. I'm hungry too and I need some more coffee."

"OK, I don't drink coffee unless I have to but I love Diet Coke. A Diet Coke and chicken biscuit for breakfast. Outstanding!"

As we sat down he bowed his head and closed his eyes for a couple seconds. I smiled when he lifted his head. "I'm not used to seeing a guy pray who doesn't want to be preached at."

"You ever met anybody liked being preached at? I know my life is FUBAR and I know it's my own fault. I damn sure don't need someone else to tell me that."

"Foo … bar?"

"Fucked up beyond all recognition. It's a military term."

I laughed out loud, "That's hilarious. Were you in the military?"

"54th Air Cav out of Ft. Hood. You can ask the rest of it."

"The rest of it?"

"You know … the usual stuff. How long was I in the

military? Was I in the war? Iraq? Afghanistan? How'd I get homeless, all that."

I was silent. My silence was about me. It was born of not knowing what to do next. How much did I really want to know? The more I knew the more I might be haunted by this guy. The more I might get tangled in anything past the next hour. *I drive by his corner every day.* My silence was about self-protection. But then my heart got the better of me.

"Do you want to talk about it?"

His blank stare was unreadable. It was as if the human part of him had temporarily shut down, and his soul was hanging behind a door like an old suit in a closet. I don't know what brought him back, but he resurrected with joy. "Yes. Outstanding! I can practice for my meeting. Practice, practice, practice. You're not really supposed to practice ... but I still get nervous at 'em. Which is weird, 'cause I'm sure not nervous about talking any other time. I love to talk."

"Meeting?"

"Yeah, you know AA ... Alcoholics Anonymous ... where you talk about your shit so you can stay sober?"

I realized he was waiting for my recognition. "Oh, yeah, so you're sober? That's good."

"Twenty-nine days this time but I've been before. I made it to seven hundred fourteen last time but I fucked it up. Michele and I were doing good and then she screwed up her ankle. They gave her some Percocet and that was it. I love me some Percocet now. I crush 'em up and snort 'em. Gotdamn, that's a good rush!"

The two high school girls next to us got wide-eyed and headed for the door. He realized he had shouted, sheepishly got up and took a last bite as he rose. He wrapped what was left and stuck it in his coat pocket. "I'm scaring the neighbors. We oughta get going."

I had ordered two chicken and biscuits and was going to leave the uneaten one and just take the coffee before I realized how precious that food might be later to Will. I wrapped it up. As we walked out I said, "Hey Will you want my second one? I won't ever eat it."

"Oh ... oh, oh, oh, yeah. Thanks man, thanks ... Should I keep going?" He pointed at the street. "I think I'm talking too much. Am I talking too much?" He pointed again.

"No, man. I promised you a pair of boots. Rock on, buddy. Talk all you want."

I clicked the fob on my key chain and started the car. He rattled on in rapid fire about a helicopter shot down, shrapnel in his neck, the gotdamn BTI, OxyContin, Iraq, the long spiral down, living in a hooch under I-65, heroin, God, and sobriety in no recognizable order for the next ten minutes. His life really was FUBAR.

The ladies at the Army/Navy store gave us cautious looks from behind the high counter. As we headed to the shoes, the store speakers crackled, "Jeff, can you head to footwear?"

I knew our prompt service had to do with the way Will looked. Jeff was well over six feet and a hundred pounds over what he needed to be. I assumed he was the most intimidating human in the store, but he smiled and asked how he could help us. I glanced at Will who had a look of panic on his face. I had no clue as to what was triggering the panic but I knew it was visceral. *Keep the situation moving, Josh.*

"I'm betting you're Jeff. I'm Josh. This is Will. He needs a new pair of boots."

Will didn't speak. He walked directly to a pair of greenish gray military-looking hiking boots. "Those. Those right there. Yes sir, right there. Gore-Tex, lightweight, waterproof, breathable. Plus the color reminds me not to go backwards. I gotta move forward."

Jeff the clerk just stared at him then asked what size. I didn't ask Will what he meant either but now I wish I had.

We got extra socks for the new boots. I grabbed a package

of long underwear on our way to the counter and asked if the large would fit.

"You don't have to do that. That's too much, too much."

"Think of me like the Methodists."

Will stared at me. His eyes still showed life but I could tell his soul was trying to run back into that closet for protection. He shook it off. "OK."

In the car I asked, "Hey, you said you were twenty-nine days sober, right?"

"Yes sir, twenty-nine days. No drugs, no alcohol."

"That means tomorrow's kind of a big deal."

"Yep, I get my chip. The red one. But this ain't my first one."

"Yeah, you talked about it earlier. About Michelle. Was she your wife?"

He looked out the window and we drove in silence. I didn't push it.

As I turned onto Sixth, he looked over at me and in a matter-of-fact, report-to-a-superior-officer's voice said, "I had two Michelles. The first was my daughter who is seventeen and last I heard is a senior in high school living somewhere in Alabama. I have not seen her in thirteen years. Her mama divorced me while I was in Iraq, second tour. My other Michelle got sober with me. She's the one who broke her ankle. We actually had an apartment for more than a year. I lost her to the drugs … I mean, I mean … I don't know where she is. I stayed on the trail of staying high for the last ten months … she disappeared from Bridgetown maybe four months ago … but … tomorrow I get my chip."

I put on my emergency flashers to help Will get his papers and backpack settled at the corner. I handed him a twenty and he tried to refuse it. I told him a deal is a deal and that I hoped to see him tomorrow on my way to work.

"Oh yeah, man, oh yeah. This is my corner. I could stay at the Methodists 'til eight but I get out early 'cause rush hour is a money maker, Mr. Baker, money maker. Plus I got my new boots!"

We both laughed and I pulled away toward my warm office. Work was a cyclone of phone calls, emails, and Excel spreadsheets. Still, I could not help but be distracted by my time with Will. It chased me most of the day with the mix of emotions that go with doing something good for someone, but knowing the job is incomplete and you can't finish it. I made a lot of assumptions. I made a lot of excuses. I asked a lot of questions. They rolled through my brain 'til they roiled in my gut.

They followed me home and I talked through it with Gina over a glass of wine after the girls were in bed. She kissed me across the table as we got up and said, "Honey, you did more than most people ever do. I'm proud of you."

My thoughts kept me awake long after Gina was out, thoughts that made me walk down the hall in the dark to watch my two little daughters lay there so innocently sleeping. I envied their peacefulness. Could Will even remember any of that innocence or had war, heroin, and homelessness beat it out of him?

Moving forward, not backward.

I laid back down in bed, overcome with emptiness. I prayed for my wife, my two daughters, my folks back in Texas, and finally for Will, then drifted off to sleep.

Will wasn't on his corner this morning.

Listen to "Belmont and Sixth," from the album
For You to See the Stars by Radney Foster.

Slow Dance

"Your hair was all done up pretty like Grace Kelly in that Hitchcock picture we saw at the Rita. You were the most beautiful thing I'd ever seen, sweetheart. Even though we'd made out in the back of my folks' Bel Air a dozen times, I was so shy 'bout pinnin' that corsage on your dress. You remember how bad my hands were shakin'? Your mama had to come help me out. It makes me laugh now." He dropped his head and his shoulders shook out a silent laugh.

"Would you look at that Bougainvillea? Honey, our water bill must be sky-high. They sure as hell won't grow out here in West Texas without you watering 'em. I'm sorry I cussed, darlin' … I know you don't like it. Lordy, they are beautiful."

She looked up from her lunch, "They are pretty, aren't they."

"Beautiful as you that prom night. That night … that night was the biggest full moon I've seen before or since. They had the doors open to the gym and you and I danced under it when the band played 'Love Me Tender.' You remember? I tell you what …"

His voice trailed off as he sat mesmerized, looking away at the white stucco wall latticed and almost completely covered with the shock of scarlet.

She had lost his attention but knew she would win it back. She had had a mysterious hold on him since the first time they met and she knew it. She took a sip of iced tea and stood up from the table. She didn't speak, just touched his shoulder with her fingertips. He put his hand on top of hers.

"They are a wonder, aren't they?" He turned his head, took her in, and smiled, then focused his attention back at the wall.

"They're the wildest red color. Wildest of any flower I've ever seen."

"Wild like you and me, Julia Ann." He winked.

She rolled her eyes. "Oh, stop."

"But I wasn't talking about the flowers. It's those two hummingbirds. First I've seen this year. They are the wonder. They fly up from Panama and Mexico. They cross 500 miles of open water in the Gulf to get here. People used to say they hitchhiked on the backs of migrating geese but that's just an old wives tale."

William H. Bell could talk a mesquite tree stump up out of the hard dry ground, especially back in his bourbon drinking days. He was a big dreamer and while he was not the smartest boy in Del Rio, no one would ever out work him. He was funny. He was sweet on Julia Ann Worley from the day he laid eyes on her in the fifth grade. He was not the first boy to exclaim to his mama that he was going to someday marry the girl he met on the first day of school, but he is the only man I ever knew who had the tenacity to pull it off. He was determined to win her heart. It took him 'til our senior year, but he did it.

"Are you getting tired?" she asked. His mind had wandered again to God knows where and shut down his tongue after he had told her everything he knew about ruby-throated hummingbirds. She had cleaned up the table from lunch and was standing behind him. The day was beginning to warm.

"Should I take you in to lay down for a nap?"

"Well now Julia Ann, what kinda man could turn down that offer?"

She indulged him with a laugh as she shook her head, "Mr. William Bell! You are one flirty old man but you know darn good and well that ain't happenin' and I have work to do." She walked him inside, down the hall, and made him comfortable on the bed. She turned off the lights and dimmed the venetian blinds but not so much that the room was completely dark. She said, "I'll wake you in a while and get you some tea," but he had already drifted off.

I am told I met Will in my first month of life. Our mothers were best friends and we therefore became playmates nearly everyday 'til we started first grade. We have been friends more than seven decades. Though neither of us can remember its beginning, the friendship was crafted by playing in sprinklers and ruling the world on bicycles at nine, baptized by stolen beers behind barns at fifteen, sealed as I handed him the ring he put on Julia Ann's finger, burnished as I helped bear their child, John, to his infant grave, and challenged as he walked me through three divorces. We have traveled ground tougher than any West Texas has to offer and outlived mothers, fathers, and siblings. We are now stripped of pretense as his mind has wandered into a pasture where no one but God can follow.

He woke as she threw open the curtains with the bright morning sun blasting through the windows. "Julia Ann, good morning. Well, you look as fresh as a daisy. Why did you let me sleep in? We are gonna go to rack and ruin if you let me miss my alarm any more." He laughed until he coughed and then settled after she sat him up rubbing his back. "Must be 'cause I was dreaming of you all night," he choked out.

She smiled. "I've got breakfast and coffee. If you want a cup of coffee first, I can keep your breakfast warm a little while. Will that work?"

"You spoil me, Julia Ann."

She had brought him tea and a couple cookies the afternoon before and he had begged her to stay in last night, but she had had a nutrition class to go to so he'd had to suffer with having dinner by himself with the news on the TV for company. She was happy he hadn't remembered and complained this morning. She liked that he woke up happy, happy to see her.

He was quiet and she was busy in the mornings. It was their usual routine but they both looked forward to lunchtime. For whatever reason, it took Will that long to gather enough of the elusive strength he needed to cut through the fog. They would go outside, sit in the shade, and he would talk. She would listen and find joy in getting a glimpse of the man he used to be.

"Julia Ann, I believe this is the prettiest spring we've had in years. You remember how we were still in the drought our senior year. My folks almost went broke my junior year, and Daddy talked about selling out and moving to Houston. Sure glad that didn't happen or I'da never won you over ... but you've heard that story a thousand times." He glanced sideways at her, his eyes lit up and he smiled, "You mind if I tell it again?" He winked.

She rolled her eyes at him. "You go right ahead."

"I fell in love with you on the first day of school when I saw you eating lunch by yourself in fifth grade. I was hypnotized by you, the new girl with auburn hair. I pushed up my glasses and told you your hair was pretty and asked you if you wanted to play checkers. Lisa May Hawkins said, 'Will Bell get away from that girl, you're gonna scare her to death.' All the girls at her table laughed. But you played checkers. You got to be friends with all those girls soon enough, but you never made fun of the shy boy with glasses. 'Course you also didn't pay any attention to me 'til our junior year in high school, but you were never mean. I swear honey you don't have a mean bone in your body and as ..."

He stopped and she knew he'd wandered into silence again. She knew it would tire him to talk more but felt it was good for him to retrieve his mind from whatever ditch it had careened into. She'd take him in for his nap soon enough, but she wanted to hear more. So, she goaded him. "You're gonna wear yourself out telling all those old stories."

He returned from whatever place had stolen his mind and smiled that sheepish, boyish grin she loved so much. "You are not much of a liar, Julia Ann. You like hearing 'em too, don't ya?"

"I do. Go on."

"Girl, whatever convinced you to let me kiss you backstage when we were in 'Oklahoma' together? All these years later I'm still not sure how the hell I pulled it off. I'm sorry sweetie, I know you don't like it when I cuss but it's true. I still can't believe it. I know what it is. I know ... you thought I's cute, didn't ya. I had to take my glasses off to be in the play and you thought there's a handsome fella underneath those horned rims. Didn't ya, didn't ya?" He looked straight at her waiting on a response.

"Well ... you are handsome."

"I ... knew it. But for the life of me I don't know how I got the courage to do it. We were standing there whispering backstage, waiting on our entrance. We'd been there a dozen times or more. Close, 'cause there was hardly any room. I looked at you and knew you wanted me to kiss you. It was your eyes ... the way you held your head, the way you were breathing slow ... like you were holding something back. But right then, right then I knew. So I kissed you. We kissed a long time." He laughed, "You remember, we almost missed our cue."

He stopped. Her eyes began to glisten but she held herself together. He was looking at her and almost spoke but his focus moved past her. Not to the flowers behind her but to some other domain where neither she nor anyone else was welcome.

"Do you want me to take you in for your nap now?" He nodded in response and she began to help him up from his chair.

Like most godfathers, I thought that my title was merely an honorary one because his daddy and I had been such good friends. I could not have predicted the way in which that beautiful little boy and his death would bind me even further to Will and Julia Ann. The term sudden infant death syndrome did not exist in 1964 in our West Texas border town. It shook everyone we knew. If there was a word for the kind of depression that a couple goes through when losing a baby, I was unaware of it. I thought of it as hell. It was dark. Will drank too much whiskey and God knows I helped him. That is, until the day Julia Ann walked into my office at the bank, looked me square in the eye, and said, "I've already lost my child and I'll be damned if I'm gonna lose my husband." I was dumbfounded and stood up wordless. "He loves you, Ben. He'll listen to you." She turned and walked out. No one had ever spoken that plainly to me in my life.

That Saturday I played nine holes of golf with Will. I played terrible, with my concentration clouded all during the round as I wondered how and what to say to Will. Fishing for the keys to his car he asked me, "What's been eating at you?"

I told him how Julia Ann had come to see me. Told him her exact words. He looked down at the hard caliche parking lot, kicked a rock, and said, "I'll be seein' ya." He never took a drink again.

Will and Julia Ann were there when I married Martha Peterson. She and I loved each other enough to have two daughters but never enough to be kind to one another. While we verbally tore apart our marriage, our girls would hide down the street at the Bell's. I thank God my girls saw in Will how a real man ought to treat a woman. They certainly never learned it from me. When Martha and I called it quits everyone breathed a collective sigh of relief. Julia Ann helped me figure out how to be the best

Dad I could from a different house. My daughters have grown up to be fine, intelligent, loving women. I have a great relationship with them, their husbands, and my grandkids. I owe all of that to Will and Julia Ann. Though they were never able to have any more children after John, they were the best parents I ever knew.

"Sweetheart, you look a little tired today. You work your fingers to the bone. Hmm ... doting on me. I do like it that I can get you to sit still and eat lunch. Talk. Well, I probably do more of the talkin' than I should but you put up with it." He paused, turned to her, and stared. At first she thought he was lost because of the silence. But this stare was different. His eyes were engaged, not without focus. There was no sign of the blankness when he was gone.

"Does it hurt?" he asked.

"What ... does what hurt?"

"Well, I know it hurts when I think about losing John. I know that pain will never go away for either of us. But ... but does it ... hurt that ... we could never have any more children?"

She was silent. She didn't really have an answer and he sensed she could not reach through her fear of saying the wrong thing.

"Well it wasn't for lack of trying!" He looked at her sideways, ducked his head, and cocked an eyebrow hoping humor would bring her smile back. It worked.

She shook her head and laughed.

"Whew boy! That trying, that was something. And I seem to remember that when we got to where the doctors told us their miserly thoughts on the matter, we kept right on a goin'."

She furrowed her brow and shook her head but her eyes were laughing. He knew he'd won her back.

I see Will twice a week and we play cards or checkers. He's still got it. For reasons beyond any worthwhile explanation, that part of his mind is crackerjack. I think it's because he's so competitive. And no amount of age or God damned mental dilapidation will ever beat it out of him. We get together mostly Wednesdays during the week and pick a funny article to read from the paper. On Sundays, I read through the bulletin from church and give the play by play as if recounting a baseball game. He listens without response. Then we get down to business. It is what old friends do.

I had not seen Will in almost two weeks. My daughters and their families had gone in together on a large condo on Rosemary Beach, and Grandpaw's presence was required. I missed a call from Dr. Sullivan and he left the message that he had some interesting news about Will. Mr. Carver, since you have power of attorney over Mr. Bell's affairs, this is information you will need to know," were the last words of his message. I called back and frustrated his nurse with a deluge of questions she was unable to answer when Dr. Sullivan was unavailable. I became determined to be home to see Will on Monday.

"It is mighty cool for the first week of June in Del Rio, Julia Ann. You'd think we moved up to Alpine or Marfa."

She had moved the patio furniture to the dappled shade and sun of a crepe myrtle tree. Will sat with a sweater over his Oxford cloth shirt and she thought how it made him look older, but she could still see through to the young man inside of him. He was still a charmer. She loved the way he tried so hard to make her laugh.

"Do you want me to move you further in the sun or get you a blanket?"

"No, no, this is perfect. Plus your smile is brighter than the sunshine. That'll keep me warm. Sounds sappy I know. But you know me." He laughed. "But then again after sixty-one years together you ought to. Only fifty-eight of that married, but I never thought of that day as anything but confirming to the rest of the world that you owned my heart. I had given you that years before and after that prom night there would never be any gettin' it back from you.

"You were so calm that night. I wasn't sure what was going to happen and I was so nervous and excited about the possibilities I thought I was gonna drive off the road on the way out to my folks lake house. You were laughing at me.

"When I saw you in the moonlight after I'd taken your dress off, I was shakin' like a leaf. You just kissed me, ran your fingers up through my hair, and pulled me to you. You knew you were gonna give yourself to me that night. I believe you knew I was never gonna leave you."

He laughed again and winked at her. "I mean hellfire we did it twice. I didn't even know that was possible." She blushed and he saw. His eyes lit up. "Sorry I cussed baby, but that night is worth cussin' about. You were so beautiful …. It was so beautiful."

His eyes glistened, a tear rolled down his left cheek, and he reached in his pocket for his handkerchief. She buried her face in her hands as she cried. He wiped his tear and gave her the handkerchief.

"You keep it baby. You're gonna make … a mess of … it … any …" His mind slipped out to wherever it wanders.

I rounded the corner, looked into Will's room, and saw he wasn't there and started to look for a nurse up at their station. I felt the metallic taste in my mouth and the sweat on the back of my neck that comes to me now when anxiety hits. I calmed down at the sight of a familiar face.

"Hey Mr. Carver," said Bette, the head nurse. "Mr. Bell is down in the courtyard. We've got a new LVN and she's been taking him down there on her lunch break almost every day. Dr. Sullivan has said it's been great for him. He's much more communicative."

I looked at the woman as if she had just spoken a foreign language. I could not comprehend what she was saying. I did not dig any deeper for fear that hope would once again prove to be a worthless charade. Hope, in Will's case, was an emotion I could no longer afford to feel. I headed down the stairs.

Will was seated at the far end of the courtyard under a tree staring into the abyss. The nurse sitting quietly next to him was a redheaded young woman with almost translucent pale white skin. She could not have been more than twenty years old. As I got closer I could tell she'd been crying. Despite her swollen eyes and ruddy cheeks she was striking and could have been Julia Ann's twin pulled half a century forward in time.

"Will?" I called out as I crossed the courtyard. "It's me, Ben."

Will sat in his usual silence and the girl looked up.

I said, "I'm Will's friend, Ben Carver," and put out my hand.

Will looked at us both as if he were a schoolboy reaching for an answer to a math problem. The girl stood up wiping her hands on her scrubs. "Yes sir, Dr. Sullivan told me about you and how you take care of things. I'm sorry I'm such a mess. Mr. Bell was just telling me an emotional story. Weren't you, Mr. Bell?"

Will looked at the girl, smiled at her, and said, "I'm tired."

I stood in shock as my jaw went slack, staring at Will. The nurse asked him, "Do want me to help you get settled for a nap?"

"That's a good idea … Ben, it's good to see you but I'm tired."

I was too stunned to speak but then caught myself. "It's good to see you too, Will." The young nurse and I helped Will up. "Would you like help getting him back to his room?" I asked.

"Sure, then we can talk after Mr. Bell is settled."

I sat in a small waiting room holding a cup of coffee and gripping the arm of the chair, white knuckled, while the young nurse got permission to spend a few minutes with me away from the floor. She came in and introduced herself as Caitlyn O'Brien. She had only been hired a few weeks before and would be here all summer, but was headed back to school in the fall to get her RN. She explained that three days after she started, Will had begun to speak to her and ask her questions. All the other nurses were shocked by it. Dr. Sullivan had said that was a good sign and had gotten the head nurse to arrange her shifts to have her care for Mr. Bell every day she was on.

"I started taking him out to get some fresh air on my lunch hour."

"That's very kind of you."

"Sir, I don't mind. He reminds me of my Papaw out in Big Spring. Plus he's such a big flirt, it's cute."

I shook my head slowly, trying to understand what she had said.

"Anyway, that's when he started talking more. Really talking. Telling stories. But it exhausts him.

"Dr. Sullivan told me to keep him talkin', no matter what. "Mr. Carver, did you know Julia Ann? Mr. Bell has called me that from the very beginning and I've just never corrected him. I didn't have the heart to. Whoever she was, he loves her. I pray to God someday I meet a man that would love me that deep and true. I think ... I hope I haven't done something wrong ... but he thinks I'm Julia Ann."

I stared at the young miracle worker. I could not hold back tears but slowly found my voice. "You look just like her. She was Will's high school sweetheart and his only love. She was a special woman. They were married almost sixty years."

I had to stop a moment, overwhelmed. I closed my eyes and finally spoke.

"She died three years ago. When cancer took Julia Ann I think Will gave up caring whether he remembered anything ever again. He hasn't spoken a word since. Not until today, not as far as I knew ... but I think you and he have been talking a while."

Those of us not embittered by life are lucky. I don't know how that happened for me but it did. My friendship to Julia Ann gave it to me. I lost so much, including Will's mind when I lost her. But I am not bitter.

Death gives us a miraculous gift, the gift of a broken heart. It takes courage to love because that's what love does. It breaks hearts. Your heart may get broken simply because another person stopped caring for you but that is just the learning curve. The real bonds between friends, family, and lovers that last decades or lifetimes make us who we are. My love for Will and Julia Ann broke me. It should have, otherwise it would never have been real.

The trick is to know that there are no points at which we stop loving, only those points at which we can no longer communicate it. I believe we pour out emotion to those we love from our souls, even if our minds are cluttered and clouded or our bodies so enfeebled and diseased that we can no longer show it. Those who hold us dear are left with fleeting glimpses of the passionate people we used to be. It is up to them to keep faith that love is hidden in the hollowness of what is left of us.

I have a lot of faith in Will Bell.

Listen to "Rock and Roll Slow Dance," from the album For You to See the Stars by Radney Foster.

Requiem

I always slept like a rock after we'd made love. The kind of dreamless nothingness that rests your body so thoroughly that it renews you soul deep. I was jolted from that blissful state at dawn that Sunday morning by the "slunk" of the deadbolt and I instinctively reached across the bed.

She wasn't there. "Sylvia?" I called out. "Sweetheart?" No answer. *OK, that's odd.*

I heard a bump and a rustling of something and the slight creek of the springs on the screen door, but never heard it close. My training took over and I slowly put on a pair of boxers and quietly slid open the drawer in my nightstand, lifted my 9mm automatic out and laid the holster on the bed.

OK. An intruder is very unlikely to try our house at daylight. Then again, they aren't usually very smart. She could just be up early piddling with something in the front ... but she always sleeps in on Sundays.

"Sylvia? Babe? Where are you?" I quickly put on the jeans

and T-shirt she'd peeled off of me while kissing, licking, and biting my skin last night between sips of red wine. I stuck the 9mm in my waistband.

From the end of the hallway I could see the driveway through the screen door. Sylvia was dressed and loading a suitcase into the Pontiac. I couldn't understand what I was seeing. It didn't make any sense.

I walked through and down the steps. I said, "Hey, sweetheart, do you need help with that? What's going on? Is your family OK?" Her look of panic was something I'd seen many times but never on her face, the panic of being caught in a lie. I'd seen it on the faces of crime suspects when I'd laid out the evidence against them in an interrogation room.

Most criminals are lousy actors and even worse at lying. Even as they try to play it cool with their voice and body language, I can see the fear that being trapped by the pile of evidence before them puts in their eyes. Sylvia had no idea how many times I've seen it before. I knew at that moment what was happening but didn't want to believe it. *She's leaving me.*

She stared at me, voiceless. I knew not to ask any further questions because she wasn't ready to talk yet. As a homicide investigator for fifteen years, I'd learned when they're ready to talk. You can't rush it.

"Come back inside, babe. Let me make you a cup of coffee." I held the screen door open as she walked up the drive in silence. She kissed my cheek when she passed.

I put the 9mm on the closet shelf next to my service weapon and briefcase and moved into the kitchen where my girlfriend was already making coffee and clearing the table from the night before. "Babe, let me do that. I said I'll make you coffee … relax a little bit, have a seat."

It was strange how the fear of losing her was shoved to the back of my brain and my heart rate dropped. I instinctively went into "crime scene" mode … dispassionate, curious, searching for things out of place. I had a death to investigate. The death of our relationship.

Trust me, everybody wants to tell their story, even the dead, particularly the dead. My job is to ask questions and listen carefully to people's stories. I knew that the dead body of Sylvia's feelings for me were right there in the room and I was about to work this like any other crime scene.

"Are your folks OK? Is Gracie OK?" I asked softly. She whispered, "They're fine, babe," as if admitting defeat. I poured coffee from the pot and added sugar to mine, cream to hers. I took a sip. I sat down across the table instead of next to her. "Are you giving the suitcases to Goodwill?"

She laughed and said, "You know too much already."

We had begun.

"I'm a good cop. Those suitcases are heavy. You got a body in one of 'em?" She smiled, but wouldn't look at me as she shook her head. "Don't make me laugh, babe." She had her hands around the coffee mug and I slid mine across to put around hers. She pulled hers back before I touched her. "Please, don't make this hard."

I let out a breath. "Whatever this is, it's hard. Might get better later, might not ... but this right here, it's hard and there ain't no gettin' around it."

I got up and put bread in the toaster so I could ask questions without making eye contact. Sometimes, it's easier for people to tell their story when they don't have to look at you. "This comes down to some basic information, babe. Where ya headed? With whom? And for how long?"

She looked sideways at me; her head still hung down over her coffee and said, "Is this a discussion or an interrogation?"

The toast popped up. I laughed and shook my head. "You sleep next to a murder cop for three years, I guess you learn a thing or two."

Every investigator has a preferred method for getting information from a suspect or a witness. Some guys use intimidation and fear. The person in your custody is already scared, disoriented. An aggressive tone of voice, an air of hostility, pissing off the suspect, and the explanation of the penalty for lying to police coupled with intentionally lengthening the process can be effective. It never worked for me. Perhaps it's because my physical size, the tone of my voice and demeanor never intimidated anyone, or maybe I have never been a good enough actor to pull it off. If the suspect knows you are acting, they'll never hand you the truth. I discovered that conversation and listening, thoroughly, were my best tools.

People have the hardest time not talking to you when you sit across from them quietly in an empty room. A lie has a piece of the truth in it. If they know what happened, even if they lie to you, they are handing you more pieces of the puzzle with every word.

We both knew the end of this story. It was never Sylvia's style to approach a problem straight on, but I wanted her to tell me the truth as much as she was able, so that her leaving wouldn't hang over me like some unsolved case. She had already told me more than she wanted without words but the detective in me wanted to compile the evidence, connect the dots, discover the motive, and nail the confession. This time however our hearts, as well as our lives together, were at stake. I didn't know if my dogged persistence as an investigator would help or hurt but it was deep in me. We were two soloists weaving melancholy streams of notes together, slowly, avoiding the crescendo the truth would bring. This was a requiem and the melody and the emotions it would dredge up were all that were left to discover.

"Why don't you start with where you're going. That might be the easiest to talk about."

She looked straight at me for the first time and said, "Colorado. I need to … I was hoping to get to New Mexico before dark."

"Well, that certainly beats San Antonio in August. It's cool up there in the mountains. Maybe I could get some time off and meet you up there." She sighed as I walked to the fridge and mumbled, "That's not a good idea."

"Come again?" I asked as I turned around with eggs, butter, and salsa. She stared straight at me and raised her voice. "I said, that's not a good idea." I looked back at her, lowered my voice, and quietly, matter of factly spoke to her the way I had to hundreds of other suspects. "You were going to leave without saying goodbye or tell me where you were going." It was a statement of fact and it hung there, empty, while I started making eggs.

When you start in the homicide division, they tell you that you only have so many murder scenes in you. It might be one or ten or ten thousand. The thing of it is, you don't know the number. No one does. I'd been at it long enough to see some guys hit it. They walk in to the scene and walk right back out. Some get super calm, some panicky and start to shake. Some cry. Some throw up. Each person handles it differently, but there is something deeply human that lies underneath his or her initial reaction. Their soul tells them they've seen too much death, too much of our unspeakable cruelty to one another. I hadn't hit my number yet but sooner or later I would. We all do.

So many homicides are in places familiar to the victim and committed by people they know intimately. Husbands, wives, lovers, friends, business partners, or family are often the assail-ant. Not all dead bodies are found in unusual circumstances, but when they are, it's my job to figure out what happened and if a crime has been committed. It is surprising to see how often the answer is apparent from the initial observation of the scene. A tremendous amount of questions are answered by where the body is found; its position, wounds, temperature, blood loss and dozens of other factors tell a story. Accidents and suicides are more common than most people realize and if I determine that's what happened, then I'm done except for the paper trail. If it looks like the death was on someone else, then I go to work. If I build enough plausible evidence to make a case and believe I'm right, I give that evidence to a District Attorney for the State of Texas. Mostly, they get an indictment and usually a conviction or a plea, depending on mitigating circumstances and the lawyers involved. For better or worse, that's how the system works. My job is to work the system on behalf of the dead.

After the longest of silences she said, "I sent you an email, telling you I'm fine but not to come looking for me. I need some space." I put a plate in front of her; an over easy egg on toast with some salsa picosa on top. It was one of her favorites but she didn't touch it.

"You thought leaving that mystery lying there would make an investigator not come looking for you? Babe, for a guy like me that's not a 'give me some space' message, that's a challenge."

"I thought I could do this ... but I can't."

"Do you mean leave or stay?"

"I thought I could be a cop's girlfriend, a cop's wife even, but I can't."

"I never bring the job home, babe."

"No, you don't." She sighed and cut into the egg but didn't eat. "You don't brood, you don't talk about what you've seen or if it bothers you. You come home happy."

"I am happy. I get home and I'm happy to see you, to kiss you, to forget my day. Make dinner together, watch a movie, make love. What's wrong with that?"

"You killed a guy!"

Then I got it. She'd hit her number. She'd never even been to a crime scene but she'd hit her number.

Most cops never fire their weapon, other than on a gun range, in their entire law enforcement career. I am one of the exceptions to that statistic. On August 5 at 7:42 a.m. I was called to a crime scene with Scott, my partner. Neighbors had heard gunshots early that morning and called the police.

They had found a locked front door and no one responded to their knock or police announcement. A dog could be heard whimpering inside and the back door was unlocked. With a "shots fired" call they figured it was better to enter the house and worry about legal technicalities later. What they found inside was a four-year-old girl wearing a Disney Princess nightgown, lying in a twin bed with four bullet holes in her little body. She had been shot while sleeping. Little children look so innocent and peaceful when they are asleep. I'd had the joy of watching my sister's kids sleep many times after singing them a song 'til they drifted off. Killing a child like that is beyond my or most people's understanding.

That little girl never knew anything about her death. Her mother, however, was not so fortunate. The first shot hit her in the shoulder and the second in the abdomen as she was running down the hallway toward her baby. She had continued to crawl toward that child as three more rounds were fired into her back, a fourth missing her. She had crawled a good ten feet leaving a smeared trail of blood. Her assailant had emptied the magazine. It was personal. The autopsy would determine that she was pregnant.

By the time Scott and I arrived a full on manhunt was taking place through the neighborhood and an all-points bulletin put out on the husband. Having the number of officers on site that these situations attract is more of a pain in the ass than a blessing. Not that we didn't appreciate the help, but that many people tend to muck up a crime scene. Plus the noise and chaos of it all makes it harder to think. I insist on a quiet crime scene when possible. Within an hour of gathering evidence from the victims, I was searching the rest of the three-bedroom ranch.

I don't really blame the patrolmen who were initially dispatched to 417 Alameda Drive. They had attempted to secure the crime scene as thoroughly as any trained cop logically could, but it was not secure.

The garage was filled with the normal junk associated with a young working family. As I entered though, I smelled a very distinct odor, sweet yet antiseptic. Ether. "Damn it to hell," I whispered, and backed out twenty feet from the open garage door before notifying one of the uniformed officers to tape off the garage and not let anyone in there. I moved even farther out to call the narcotics division, knowing that the static electricity from using your cell phone can ignite volatile liquids.

Peripheral vision is an odd thing for me. It is where the clues hide, light dances, and demons sleep. It's where I usually see what to the rest of humanity looks normal but to me is intrinsically out of place. It can be both a blessing and a curse. As someone was answering my call at narcotics, something in my peripheral vision made me drop my phone, look left, and reach for my service weapon even before I heard the report of the handgun or saw the flash from the shadows of the garage. I squared and aimed two rounds at a shadow that by then I was sure was a human being. The shadow's second round went off but was not aimed. It was merely the physical reaction of his finger on the trigger as two slugs entered his chest. That sound however, made me fire two more rounds at his falling body, one of which found its target.

It was then that I saw that officer Ruben Garza, the uniform I had just spoken to, was hit.

"Officer down!" are heartrending words to hear if you are a cop. They are even more disturbing to hear shouted from your own mouth. My job was to make sure the suspect I had just shot was either dead, or securely in custody, and that no other suspects were there. Even though another officer was already crouched over Ruben and calling an ambulance, I had to fight off the desire to go and check on him. I entered the garage and found the gunman's body and checked for a pulse. There was none. I searched for other suspects or victims.

The hide out/meth lab was simple and ingenious really. It was hidden in plain sight. There was an old six-foot-tall wooden shelf against the back wall of the garage. The shelves were littered with paint cans, an old cooler, boxes of Christmas lights, a toolbox, old toys, and other clutter. The bottom shelf was empty and a half a dozen cardboard boxes were collapsed and stacked against it. That shelf had a false back where a piece of the wall behind it had been removed. It opened to what should have been the crawl space below the kitchen and laundry room. A small room had been dug out, not tall enough to stand up straight in but big enough to house and hide the lab materials when not in use. Extra fans and a piece of air duct were there to remove fumes through a crawl space vent off the back of the house. Whatever cocktail of drugs, mental illness, and pure evil drove the individual I had just killed to do such unfathomable violence to his family was born in that make-shift room.

Once I knew the garage was secure, I walked toward Ruben and saw two officers and Scott, my partner, attending to him. My job was done and all that was left was to pray for Rueben. This place was no longer my crime scene. Solving any murder at this home turned meth lab would now be someone else's job. I would be under investigation for killing a suspect. It was standard procedure.

My superior officer, Joseph Birdwell, was there shortly to relieve me of my weapon. It was evidence. He offered me his weapon so I would not be unarmed in the field but I turned it down. I was taken to Methodist hospital where Ruben was headed, fighting for his life with a chest wound.

There they would draw blood to test for drugs or alcohol in my system and take me to the Office of Police Accountability to be interviewed about every detail I could recall. I would be placed on administrative leave pending the results of the investigation and would not be solving murders for ten weeks. The frustration of waiting to do my job would damn near drive me insane.

That had all taken place two years ago, and I remember my mood and anger during that leave had been a real test for Sylvia and me. I thought we had handled that rough spot pretty well and it was shortly after that we had moved in together. No more deciding who has to drive across town in the morning.

"The guy I killed was a bad guy, babe. He was shooting at me and another officer. He had killed his wife and child, and he damn near killed Ruben Garza." I poured her some more coffee and gently touched her shoulder as I put the pot back in the coffeemaker. She didn't flinch or pull away this time. She said, "You act like it's no big deal." At that point I quit acting like an investigator because I knew where this conversation was headed. "It's a big deal. Really big ... but I'm not going to sit around and wait for the post-traumatic stress to show up. I'm sure it will sooner or later, but probably not over that guy. If anything it will come because of all the other shit I've seen in fifteen years at Homicide. It kind of comes with the territory and everybody handles it differently."

"I can't handle it at all ... anymore."

"And that's why you are headed to Colorado." Those words went unanswered in the silence of that morning and neither one of us moved for the longest time. I was staring at her. She was so beautiful. She never lifted her eyes to look at me.

"Why did you make love to me last night if you knew you were leaving?" I asked. She sighed and slowly let out, "I knew you would ... would sleep really soundly. You always do after sex. I ... I didn't want to have this conversation."

"So all that wild passion was so I'd sleep and you could sneak away without a word?"

"It almost worked."

*Listen to "While You Were Making Time," from the album
For You to See the Stars by Radney Foster.*

Another Dragon to Slay

The Old Man hunkered down as deep as he could into a corner of the trench before he lit the cigarette. A sniper drone would have to be in one small exact spot to see the heat marker.

It was worth the risk. He loved the heat of the cigarette in this cold and there was something about the tradition of it. Real tobacco was hard to come by but he had his ways. He had a picture of his father smoking with his buddies in Afghanistan in '04.

His own first smoke was decades later, at the battle of Leon, Mexico. His sergeant had told all the newbies to bum a smoke after their first firefight. Nicotine slows down the dopamine crash.

"Old Man, put that gotdamn contraband out before you get us all blown to hell." Sergeant Robert Mota buried the butt in the half-frozen mud. "Yes sir, Captain!"

Captain Barton tossed a pack of gum to Mota. "How did you get in this man's army anyway?"

Sergeant Mota shook his head and laughed. He tapped the Lone Star patch on his left sleeve and popped nicotine gum into his mouth. "Same way you did, sir. When Texas joined the United American Republic."

"Always wonder whether we're allowed to wear the Lone Star as an honor or a reminder we couldn't go it alone." Captain Barton was a Texan as well but unlike Mota was a First Citizen. Mota liked Barton. Unlike most 1st Cs, Barton treated everyone the same. Mota could not help but count his time left. Three more years of service and he would finally earn First Citizenship giving him the same privileges as Barton.

The margins of error for maintaining a democracy are thinner than most realize. Sergeant Mota had never fully comprehended how fragile it was. He had been born a citizen of the United States of America, which had crumbled into nothingness. He'd had freedoms as a kid he did not feel the need to worry about. The only time he thought about citizenship was to pass a standard middle school civics test. Now, he had to distinguish between the rights and privileges of others and his own. Somehow, his rights were always left wanting.

Barton scanned the western horizon and the smoke pluming off the Denver skyline. "Old Man, find that damned lieutenant of yours, the one who's supposed to be your commanding officer. Get him to headquarters at 14:00. All sergeants join us at 15:00 hours."

"You want Non-Coms at HQ, sir?"

"That's an order, Sergeant." He rubbed his temples.

"You alright, sir?"

"We'll be fine."

Non-Coms do not attend HQ meetings. Something was bent up all to hell and whatever it was Mota knew that Barton was trying to keep it from him.

Barton was the only one who called Mota "Old Man" to his face, though soldiers in his unit called him that behind his back when he made their lives hard. He didn't care. He never rode their asses out of spite, but only what was necessary to get them prepared. He had survived twenty years of war. The men of Charlie Company knew it, too.

Mota's hair had gone gray years ago but the nickname was not because of his age or appearance. He had earned it in action six years earlier in Occupied Mexico. He and then-Lieutenant Barton had figured out an end around maneuver under heavy fire that crushed an insurgency one night in the streets of Saltillo. Mota had kept the lieutenant and a dozen others from getting shot all to hell and their colonel had seen it all go down on the live video feed. The colonel told Barton, "That old man knows how to kill the enemy and get shit done. Stick with him and you might have a career in the army." The nickname had stuck.

Mota could smell 1st Lt. James D. Strayhorn's lunch from outside his bunker. He was given permission to enter and saw half a roasted chicken; an actual chicken raised above ground, served with mashed potatoes, real butter, and green beans. The last time Mota ate real food was two Christmases ago.

Strayhorn's father had been the highest bidder in the 2044 Senatorial Auction for one of the seats from the state of Alabama. The senator's position in the United American Republic gave him and his family special rights and privileges, even beyond those of First Citizens. One of those privileges was real food shipped piping hot via drone to his son on the battlefield. Mota informed his superior officer of the 14:00 meeting at HQ.

"Sir?" he cleared his throat, "Captain Barton ordered Sergeants Walker, Clementi, and myself there at 15:00 hours for briefing as well."

"That's unusual. Inform them … make sure they're there, Sergeant."

"Yes, sir."

Mota found Sergeant Walker shoring up his squad's section of the trench and silently motioned with his head over his shoulder. Walker put on the poncho to hide his body heat from a sniper drone and followed. "What's up?"

"I'm not sure ... but it can't be good."

Both men stopped and listened to the rumble of artillery in the distance.

Sergeant Clementi felt he was being watched. Behind his trench, he saw Mota and Walker standing in the muck that had once been a pasture. They were not speaking. "Ah, damn it," he whispered. He wanted to keep his men moving in this cold. "Corporal Harrison! Weapons inspection in twenty minutes. I don't want to see anyone standing around doing nothing." He pulled the hood of his poncho up over his helmet and climbed out of the trench toward Mota and Walker.

"To what do I owe the pleasure of your staring?"

Walker glanced at Mota.

"There's a meeting at HQ at 15:00 hours and we've been invited to attend by the captain."

Walker spat on the ground. Clementi mumbled, "Shit, shit, shit." The smoke and haze coming from the west grew thicker. Mota coughed and said, "Don't spook the men. Let them think we're just catching up on the latest dirty jokes rolling through camp."

Clementi looked disgusted, leaned in, and whispered, "There is not one normal fucking thing about this and no good is coming our way because of it. I take orders from my El Tee and then make them happen. Not this shit." He paused. "OK, now everybody laugh."

The three sergeants guffawed as Mota continued to check the perimeter. He stomped his feet against the cold and said, "There is nothing normal about a platoon with an El Tee that is a diamond crusted senator's son. Those people only serve for one reason. They are looking to get noticed by The President so they can make another billion dollars. I've been at this a long fucking time and ain't ever seen one within a hundred miles of a battlefield. We've been sitting out here dug in, starving Denver for four months, since he showed up. 34th Artillery starts shelling heavy three days ago along with hellfire from the air? Captain tells me NCOs are going to a meeting with brass at HQ? Shit's fixin' to fly."

Clementi kicked the frozen ground. "I do not like talking to full bird colonels. It's a good way to get caught in a crazy scheme that has nothing to do with good soldiering. A man can get blown all to hell like that."

Mota looked out over the trenches and bunkers filled with boys who had fought cold and boredom in the open plains of Colorado 'til they couldn't remember what it was like to be warm. He laughed for their benefit, then leaned in. "Do either of you have any volunteers in your squads?"

Clementi said, "Not unless you include me."

Mota looked at Walker.

"Worse, more than half of mine are conscripts. My corporals are good soldiers, though. One's a draftee—the other is five years into a six-year hitch. He's trying to get his family's 1st C status back. They got demoted to Resident when his brother got sideways with the law. It's easy to go down, hard to move up. I guess he's a volunteer of sorts."

Clementi laughed and said, "Did you tell him welcome to the club?"

"Shit, Six years? I guess if you start out a 1st C the goalposts are different ... damn sight different than if your grandfather is from Mexico." Mota spit out his gum and continued. "Well someone has cooked up something special for this outfit. Walker, can you get some skinny from 2nd and 3rd platoons without causing a fuss?"

Walker nodded.

"Get everyone and everything inspection and mobile ready. I want us all looking like bad asses 'cause I got a feeling we may have to actually move out and be bad asses tomorrow."

Mota walked toward his own makeshift HQ, and double

stepped down the ladder into the trench, "Corporals! My office now."

Sergeant Mota's "office" was a tent in a wide spot in the trench made of a somewhat bulletproof material impregnated with photovoltaic webbing as a solar energy source. Heat and light were controlled by voice command. Their unit was supposed to be outfitted with enough of these tents so that all the men would be shielded from the elements, but times being what they were, and the Republic being strapped for cash, there was only one. Mota was the senior NCO in Charlie Company and so it was his office by day and should have been his to bunk in by night. But he cared about the health of his men, and it had become an improvised sick bay on the coldest nights for any men bad off but not sent back to Ft. McCain. He rarely slept there. He informed Corporals Birrianski, Pak, and Martinez of inspection at 13:30 and that every soldier should be prepared to move out within an hour's notice from that time forward.

"This ain't a drill. Something's up and I want us prepared." They were kids like Mota had been when he first signed up and he hated not knowing what he was leading them into.

The Old Man was jonesing for a real smoke. He looked at the picture of his wife and kids. It was several years old but still his favorite, a candid from a vacation at the Grand Canyon. His son and daughter were making faces at each other and his wife was laughing. One of those goofy shots you catch after a pose. They had gone on vacation there when the Ford Foundation still maintained it and several other Continental Parks in the no-man's-land of the Rocky Mountains. Less than four years later, the political and military skirmishes between Pacifica and the UAR had closed all of those and laid waste to the Grand Canyon in a massive battle over control of Arizona. If he could survive three more years on the battlefield he and his family would become First Citizens.

Robert Mota's grandparents had been born in Mexico, but

became naturalized citizens of the old United States. Under the rules of the UAR, only those native-born for three generations were granted First Citizenship. Everyone else was Resident Citizen with no right to vote and limited property and travel rights. Sergeant Mota, his wife Angela, their children, grandchildren, and on forevermore would be Residents only, unless they met the right criteria.

There were only three ways for Residents to become 1st Cs: marry into it, purchase it, or serve in the military. For Mota, the first two were not options. When he signed up, you could get First Citizenship after serving six years. Then it was ten. Then it was more. He didn't have time today to fume about the Republic continually moving back the length of military service necessary for immigrant families to reach 1st C.

At 14:30 Mota, Clementi, and Walker waited for the transport to HQ along with all of the sergeants in Charlie Company. They all looked to Mota for guidance, not because he outranked them but because of experience. "Well, boys?" They all looked at him as he entered the Tracker ready to carry them to HQ. "It's a new day in the American Republic!" he exclaimed, mimicking The President's favorite political slogan of the last sixteen years. All the men roared with laughter, breaking the tension.

The NCOs entered HQ with a reasonable amount of trepidation. All officers were 1st Cs, and the noncommissioned officers were Residents. In or out of the military, there was always a distinction.

Each man snapped to attention upon entering the large bunker and seeing the brass. They were told by Captain Barton to be "at ease," but in this situation and in most of their interactions with 1st Cs truly being at ease was never possible. They were a different tribe.

A paunchy General Jefferson H. Tartian took the podium, looking sleepy and disheveled. Everyone snapped to attention and he implored them, "At ease, at ease." The officers relaxed and began sitting back down. The NCOs remained rigid as marble columns, their right hands at salute. The general returned their salute. "At ease, men. There is a reason you are here." He grabbed the podium as if to steady himself and launched into one of the political rants that preceded all orders.

"The City State of Denver has troubled our Christian republic for far too long, and the next forty-eight hours begins their great Final Reckoning! Too long they have thwarted our decrees. Too long they have ignored our treaties. No more will they harbor infidels and atheists. No more will they shelter our escaped prisoners and traitors leaving our country without travel privileges. Their illegal contraband and vile drugs will plague our great Republic no more. Tomorrow we crush their scurrilous philosophies, which continue to be a reckless influence on our nation's youth. No longer will the good people of Denver suffer under the immoral influences of Pacifica. We shall deliver Denver to safety and freedom. And the people said?"

"Amen!" rang out through the seated officers and men.

"Captain Barton, I am sure that Charlie Company is curious why you, your officers, and NCOs have been summoned here this afternoon." Mota could have sworn the general looked straight at him before continuing. "We have had Denver cordoned off from the outside world for months. We thank you and your men for your service here in that effort this winter. The 4th and 5th divisions as well as the 7th armored will be attacking simultaneously from the north and northwest. The invasion of Denver will commence in the next thirty-six hours. The key to that invasion's success is the stealth of a targeted spearhead here in the east. Leading that spearhead will be the 4th Special Tactical Unit."

Fuck! thought Mota. He looked down the two rows of his fellow sergeants, then across the aisle directly at Barton who shot him a quick glance.

"Charlie Company has been tasked with the honor of being the human liaison to the 4th Tactical. Lieutenant Strayhorn will be your Audio Visual Coordinator from A/V HQ at Ft. McCain."

Of course he is, Mota thought. *Now it makes sense.*

"Captain Barton, your NCOs will require special communications training beginning tomorrow morning at 08:00 hours, and you will move out under cover of darkness at 02:00 hours the following morning. Any questions?"

Mota rubbed his temples. His ears began ringing. He had seen what a Tactical Nuclear Unit could destroy. He was not anxious to see it again. Two days after the fall of Chicago, he had entered a children's hospital to be treated for radiation poisoning and have shrapnel removed from his shoulder. Of all the things he had seen in the last twenty years of war, Comer Children's was what haunted his nightmares the most.

"No? Good. Captain Barton, I'll have you coordinate the particulars of your mission with Colonel Haistings ..."

Mota got up so violently that he knocked over his chair. "Permission to speak freely, sir!"

His tone and obvious disregard for the protocol when a Resident speaks to a senior officer shocked General Tartian.

"State your name sergeant!"

Mota's career and his family's shot at First Citizenry were at risk in that instant. His life and the lives of his men outweighed his ability to tread lightly. He softened his tone but not his determination.

"Master Sergeant Robert L. Z. Mota, sir." He snapped to attention.

General Tartian looked directly at the sergeant and held the gaze letting his superiority sink in for the entire room. He finally spoke, "Sergeant Mota?"

"General Tartian, sir, I believe that ..."

"Sergeant Mota!" roared the general, "While I appreciate the fact that you have lived here on the battlefield for months, here at headquarters enlisted men are expected to speak formally to a superior officer."

Mota had been set up for the fall but he coolly took the dress down. *So this is the game we are playing.*

"It is my honor to serve the Lord our God, his servant The President, and our great United American Republic. Amen. General Tartian, your permission to speak freely."

"Permission granted."

"General Tartian, sir, with all due respect ... I believe that I am the only soldier in Charlie Company, the 3rd Battalion, 9th Division, and quite possibly the IV Corp. who has any practical experience with the 4th Tactical Unit. I fought beside them in the battle for Chicago when that ..." *He needed to choose his words carefully.* "great city was reunited with its proper home, the United American Republic. Sir, I was a member of the 2nd Battalion, 17th Armored Infantry attached to the 4th Tactical ... eight hundred men strong."

Mota bit the inside of his cheek and swallowed. He tasted blood. "I am one of the two dozen survivors from that unit. I believe I am the only one still serving in the military, sir."

The Old Man never let his glare leave the general.

"General Tartian, sir. I have no doubt about the ability of a tactical drone tank unit armed with nukes to kill the enemy ... it is everything else they kill that concerns me. In particular the men I lead."

The general strolled across the dais and back. "Sergeant, your service in Chicago was commendable and the heroism of the 2nd/17th is legendary." He stroked his chin. "Your experience here is invaluable. It is one of the reasons we have chosen Charlie to be the 4th Tactical's liaison."

Clearly, he had read Mota's file.

"We have made great strides in artificial intelligence and remote command since you last served with them in the field. It is one of the reasons we only need a company as liaison rather than a battalion."

Charlie Company is expendable, thought Mota.

He only needed one more question answered, but his life and the lives of his men depended upon it.

He cleared his throat. "Begging your pardon, sir. We NCOs are used to a chain of command. I am not used to speaking with generals. I take my orders from lieutenants and captains, sir. Will Charlie Company remain under Captain Barton's command?"

"Absolutely, Sergeant. Captain Barton, you may rearrange your company command as you see fit for this special operation."

Barton was their only hope.

Small tactical nuclear weapons have been around since the 1950s. They had originally fired from a hand held or Jeep mounted rocket. There was ancient film footage of them being tested with Attorney General Robert Kennedy attending along with the gaggle of press. The UAR had merely modernized the old stockpiles and attached them to driverless "drone" tanks, needing no human on the ground to deal with radiation. The problem was that as good as the cameras in the air were, the gamers at Ft. McCain needed eyes and ears on the ground for the tanks to be effective.

The Battle of Chicago was a long, slow series of ever weaving, bloodletting skirmishes. By May of 2041, The President's need to appear strong, and his disgust with the term "bogged down," finally overwhelmed the advice he received from his *consigliere*. He lusted after decisive victory.

The President's war room and political advisors had warned that using nuclear weapons would make the UAR a pariah nation to the rest of the world. Political theory had been that concern for human life and environmental destruction needed to be a part of the equation that went along with any military victory. Conventional wisdom predicted that sanctions, trade embargoes, and economic disaster would ensue. The President hated conventional wisdom.

The symbolic strength of the mushroom cloud and the fear it wielded was more than The President could resist. The 4th

Tactical and 17th Armored used a mountain of conventional weapons on that city and their destruction of buildings and flesh was massive. But it was the five tactical nuclear weapons that sent a message to the world.

The nukes took out a few city blocks each, along with hundreds of souls. The Old Man's battalion had been caught in the nuclear friendly fire.

Mota was assaulted with questions the moment the door to the Tracker was closed. He sat mute. Every fiber in him wanted to sneak through the perimeter, head west, and escape. It would be the easier choice. He could work his way south and west through the deserts and mountains, where the only government to speak of was the local sheriff, 'til he got to Pacifica. He could try to find his sister in San Jose and anonymously slip into a more placid life. She had predicted more than two decades earlier that the Republic of Texas would end badly, be unable to resist the UAR, and she had left for the West Coast.

Even if he was caught and shot for desertion, he would not have to face the hell of tactical nuclear weapons. He had lived through it once. He swore he would never deal with it again.

But the pull of family and brothers in arms was too strong.

He whispered, "My tent." Walker, next to him, shouted, "Listen up!" Every man turned to Mota.

"My tent, after I talk to the captain. I can't speak for your El Tee's but Barton's a good soldier. I've been from the Sandbox to Mexico to Korea with him. Let me talk to him. He knows about Chicago." He stared down the line of men. "Afterwards, my tent, by platoon. If we plan and execute well, we have a shot at walking out of this thing."

Charlie Company was supposed to be a rapid response light infantry unit and trained for it at one time. Officers above the rank of major receiving their advancement by presidential appointment changed everything. Politically loyal appointed 1st Cs, looking to guild their chests without risk or bravery required, curried favor. Deportation statistics made The President happy. He wanted a show of force, so Charlie Company and the rest of the 3rd Battalion had spent the last year guarding deportees headed to Occupied Mexico out of Camp Spencer in south Texas. It was the largest of all the deportation camps in the UAR. They had moved out to join the IV Corp in the siege of Denver as that city-state's negotiations with The President broke down and winter moved in. Mota was now sure why this assignment had fallen to them. Only one soldier in the UAR knew what really happened in Chicago.

The President was tying up loose ends.

The tracker came to a stop and Mota ordered, "Everything and everyone is to be ready to move out by tomorrow at 06:00. I don't give a good goddamn what your El Tee's say about training schedules. I've seen this movie. Get moving." He opened the door and was slapped by the cold wind.

He watched as all the lieutenants left Barton's bunker and headed to chow at the officer's mess. He knew Barton would not head that way. He was a different breed, and before a battle he would eat what the men ate. It was one of the things that made Mota respect him. With all that was required to move out, the men of Charlie Company, tonight, would scarf down meals-ready-to-eat. Captain Barton would do the same. Mota waited twenty minutes before he knocked.

"Permission to enter, sir!"

"Mota! Get your ass in here."

"Yes sir!"

"Sit down, Mota. Have you eaten?"

"Yes sir."

"Good, that's good. I knew you'd show up. Saved me the trouble of calling you here."

Barton reached into a locker and pulled out a canteen. He set it on the table and then went to another locker and pulled out two actual whiskey glasses wrapped in socks. He took out the glasses and opened the canteen. Mota could smell the alcohol and sweetness of bourbon. Barton said, "You have your contraband and I have mine."

In almost six years of serving with Barton, they had never shared anything close to this familiarity. They had been forced by the nature of the job into a strange intimacy, made brothers by the field of battle. Duty, fear, and death had bound them together, but they had always respected the boundaries of officer and enlisted man.

"Sir, I ... uh, fraternizing with an officer can cost me ..."

"Mota, shut up and have a whiskey. That's an order." Barton poured two fingers worth of whiskey in each glass.

Barton pulled a small box from a shelf and set it on the table, flipped the top open, and turned it toward Mota. "Old Man, these are long overdue." The sergeant stared down at the pair of lieutenant's bars.

"Sir, I'm not sure I understand."

"It's called a battlefield commission. I need you to have the authority of an officer. I need you to run 1st Platoon."

Mota laughed, "Sir, all due respect but I already run 1st Platoon ... and every El Tee in Charlie turns to me and pretty much does whatever I suggest. I'm not sure those help you or me in this situation." He took a sip of whiskey, felt the sting of it, closed his eyes, and let the flavor of caramel, vanilla, and apples swirl through his head.

"They mean immediate First Citizenship for you and your family. Plus, the army will give you the benefit of the doubt on your next three years. You can retire at the end of this year. That is, when we take care of this Denver ... Tactical 4th party we are about to throw. But it's your choice, you don't have to accept it."

The Old Man rubbed his chin with his thumb. Was this a bribe or consolation to his widow and children? "Is this offer from General Tartian?"

"What's your real question, Old Man?"

"I think they singled out Charlie Company because of me. I can't talk about Chicago if I'm dead. If the gamers fuck this one up, Tartian will make sure no one in Charlie survives. Do you have orders to make sure I don't make it?"

"I have no such orders. You may be right about being singled out but it doesn't matter now. That knowledge doesn't change my orders and my orders are to be eyes and ears. I was given first coordinates and protocols for each platoon. We train on their new communication gear tomorrow. But ... I was given no orders for Strayhorn. He is on his way to Ft. McCain."

Barton looked down at the lieutenant's bars and pointed to them with his glass. "Those were my idea. I was told I could arrange Charlie Company's command as I saw fit."

Barton watched as Mota pondered. Finally, he said, "Speak your mind, Mota."

"Speak my mind? Well ... hell, Captain, I'm old enough to remember a time when everyone had the same rights.

"I was a citizen of the USA. My father and my mother served in the military on a battlefield. See any women at all in uniform on this side?

"The odds were stacked against brown families like mine and we knew it ... but at least we had the same rights as everyone else. I was taught that if I busted ass I had a chance to get ahead. When I joined the Army of the Republic of Texas, I was a proud Texan ready to serve my new country. By the time Texas joined the UAR, my rights as a Citizen had been stripped from me because my grandfather was born in Mexico. Tell me Captain Barton, where are your grandparents from?"

"New Jersey, Cape May."

"Part of the Yankee Compact. So they weren't born in this country either. But you are a 1st C."

Barton's anger flared. "Sergeant, what does all this fucking history have to do with dealing with tactical nuclear weapons in thirty hours? And, surviving it!"

Mota took a slug of whiskey. "I'll tell you exactly, sir." He stared straight at the captain. "The men don't trust officers. None of my men are 1st Cs. Every enlisted man in Charlie with the exception of myself and Clementi was either conscripted out of prison or drafted. Only Residents are drafted. 1st Cs are exempt. You are a different team inside and outside of the army."

"Every one of your men would jump at this chance in life."

"Yes, sir, they would. The moment I put on those bars I'd fulfill their wildest dreams … and betray them. I'd no longer be one of them, and I need to be one of them if we are going to have any chance of surviving."

Barton sat back.

"You are the exception to that rule, sir. About officers I mean. I've known it from the time you were my lieutenant. The men are going to follow you if they think you are risking what they are … and have a plan that involves them getting home."

"Well, I'm damn sure risking what they are." Barton picked up the lieutenant's bars. "I'm gonna cut you a deal. I keep these for thirty days, but send in the paperwork now so your wife and kids are covered … no matter what. Now tell me about Chicago and what we do if some kid running a drone tank with live nuclear weapons fucks up."

Mota looked away as he felt his eyes glisten, not because of the captain's gesture and what it would mean for his family, but because of the stench of charred and mangled children in a hospital in Chicago that would never fully leave his nostrils.

He had thought about tactical nuclear weapons every day since. His self-medication for the crazies that had haunted him since May 7, 2041, was to learn everything he could about them. "I can't talk about Chicago and do my job, sir. But I can talk about the plusses and minuses of drone tanks with nuclear warheads."

"There are plusses?"

"Depends on who you are talking to. The tactical units don't have any human beings they train with to go into battle because the nineteen-year-old gamers need to not give a shit about collateral damage or friendly fire. You don't want to sit next to a guy at chow for two years you might have to vaporize to win the game."

"Win the game?"

"The kids running this cluster are all gamers. Their officers grew up gamers. The whole thing is set up as a game. They get points for ground taken, enemy destroyed, etc. They lose points for collateral damage of civilians, but not much. They are cheap. We soldiers are expensive, but just like a queen in chess ... they'll sacrifice us to win the game. The problem is there are very few points for just rolling into Denver with no resistance. They look for a fight. But then I think resistance will be heavy."

Barton put the stopper in the bottle and nestled it into a drawer. "Why do you think that, Old Man?"

"Because all the priority boarding set flew away before the siege. Everyone else there has known freedom their whole life and have no desire to wear my shoes under The President."

Barton shook his head. "Shhh, Sergeant, you can still get court-marshaled for that kind of talk."

The Old Man swallowed the last of his whiskey. "Tonight, I'll take my chances. We have to think like the enemy for a bit. We need to know the weaknesses in the game to survive the same way they do. As good as the cameras are on the drones flying over us ... we are the Tactical 4th's eyes and ears."

Barton looked at Mota and said, "And Strayhorn is in charge of the game controller."

"Strayhorn is ambitious, sir. He is also our eyes and ears over the gamers at Ft. McCain. May I be candid, sir?"

Barton laughed, "You haven't been yet?"

Mota thought about the risk of what he was about to suggest to a commanding officer. It could get him shot for treason. He tried to read this officer he had always trusted.

Fuck it. "We can manipulate his ambition. How much do you trust the good lieutenant, sir?"

"Not as far as I can throw him." Barton stared at Mota deep in thought. A grin came to his face. "He's political."

Mota grimaced, nodded his head, and laughed. "We can manipulate that, too. Let him filter every damn communication through the lens of looking good for The President. We need to study coordinates and maps tonight, sir, and we need to get Clementi in here, too, sir."

"Why Clementi?"

"His parents were raised in Denver. He may be our ace in the hole."

Barton smiled at the Old Man and said, "Just like old times down in Mexico. Go get Clementi and do it quietly. Not on a radio."

Mota braced himself for the blast of cold at the doorway, turned back to Barton, and asked, "So, tell me sir, why are we taking Denver?"

"Politics. The President wants another victory, another dragon slain to parade before the people in time for the next election."

"There will always be another dragon to slay."

The Old Man headed into the cold.

Listen to "All That I Require," from the album
For You to See the Stars by Radney Foster.

The Night Demon

There is a howling, screaming demon in my bedroom late at night. It is terrifying hellfire that is sure to curse my soul to perdition, but it is irresistible. Its one eye glows red under my bed covers and it has a lone tentacle that sucks deep into my ear to siphon off my brain. Once it has my brain, I'm afraid it will go after my heart and soul. It is rock and roll.

Daddy Jack is my granddaddy and my friends at school all think it's strange that us grandkids call him that but that is all we know to call him. He used to be a Pennycostal preacher part time but now he sells cars in Uvalde. My friends at school think we are kind of weird anyway on account of my mamaw's big hair and my sister's long dresses but we are all Pennycostal and that is how we do.

Mamaw picks us up from school 'cause Mama works at the bank and that is why the other kids see her big hair. Other ladies have big hair sometimes but not like Mamaw. Her hair is really, super big. Daddy Jack is tall and Mamaw is short but her hair makes her taller than he is.

You can get TV now in West Texas on account of the cables and Mama saved up and bought one at the furniture store. One time Daddy Jack and Mamaw came over to watch our new TV, which isn't really new but it is to us. I hid behind the couch 'cause I wanted to see if that hair could hold one of my little plastic army men, without Mamaw noticing. I snuck up super quiet and stuck one a them army men into her hair while something exciting was happening on the TV. Did you know she can hold a whole squad of six army men in there? Mamaw didn't find them 'til she went to bed that night and it apparently scared the bejesus outta her. She had to wake up Daddy Jack to help her get them all out. She called Mama on the phone and told her about it and I heard 'em laughing. Mama looked in on me and thought I was sleeping but I was playin' possum. I knew the next morning I would get a talking to but nobody was really mad and I didn't get a whipping.

Mama is Pennycostal like the rest of us and she makes sure she dresses me and my sister, Jeanie, Pennycostal but I'm not sure if she's really as Pennycostal as the rest of us. She might be only partly Pennycostal. First off, we don't have a Daddy around which ain't very Pennycostal, and she works at a bank and isn't home when we get through with school which ain't very Pennycostal, and her hair ain't as big as the other ladies in church and she bought that TV ... but the biggest reason I'm not sure she's as Pennycostal as the rest of us is that she bought the demon.

The demon is a red transistor pocket radio that was made in Japan with an earpiece that you can plug in. Mama got it for a dollar at a yard sale for my birthday. It has a speaker where everybody can hear but if you plug the earpiece in, only you hear it. 'Cept everybody else can hear it a teenie weenie bit unless you keep the volume wheel low and hide under the covers at night.

In the daytime I can only hear three radio stations on it— KDLK from over in Del Rio, XERF from Acuña, Mexico, and another station from Mexico where everything is in Spanish.

KDLK plays all kinds of music except rock and roll. Their motto is "Nice Music For Nice Folks." Boy howdy is it boring! None of their music has any thump to it at all. Even their gospel music show is boring. No thump, no sir. Not like the Holy Ghost gospel we sing at church. Whooooo boy, now that music has thump and then some. Reverend Eaglesmith has a big red Gibson electric guitar, Mrs. Worsham plays piano, and seven or eight people got tambourines, and when the music gets to thumping people start speaking in tongues and sometimes get slain in the Spirit and fall to the ground.

Now, in the daytime, XERF has gospel and some of it thumps and they got that good Pennycostal preaching that Daddy Jack likes. He'll even give the radio an "Amen" sometimes. The music on the other Mexican station thumps too and I kind of like it even though I can't understand it. At night, everything changes and I do mean everything. I can hear all kinds of stations that fade in and out from all over America. KDLK goes off the air but XERF goes wild. One time when Daddy Jack was listening to a gospel show on XERF, he said that the station was good in the daytime but late at night howling demoniacs take over and I should never listen at night. I asked, "What's a demoniac?" He said it was someone possessed by devils and you could hear 'em screaming.

For the longest time I didn't go nowhere near the end of that dial. The thought of listening to screaming demons was too scary, but I kept wanting to find music with thump and I'd inch as close as I could to 1570 on the dial. Then my curiousness got going and I inched it too far. They sure as shooting had a wolf-man on the radio! He was howlin' and a-screamin' and selling pep pills for your lingnuts that he said, "would put the zippity zing back in your zippity do." I want to ask Daddy Jack what lingnuts are and do I have any and do they need peppin' up but every time I get the chance it never seems like a good idea. He might know I was listening to the demoniacs late at night.

Right after this wolf-man creature finished up selling the lingnut pep pills he played a record by some possessed soul called Little Richard and there it was. The thump! I mean that guy was not fooling around when it came to thumping. He was screaming at Lucille to come back where she belongs with the beat banging along and it was the wildest, thumpingest music I had ever heard in my nine years on this planet. Next thing, with no pause, this wolf fella played a song called "The Wanderer" by some guys called Dion and the Belmonts. I got scared that Mama might hear and take back my radio so I turned it off lickity split. I laid there with my heart pounding and thought that station is trouble for sure. And then, it happened. "The Wanderer" would not go out of my head. I was sure it was the work of the devil 'cause it stayed stuck all night and all the next day at school. It got so stuck I had to be careful to not start singing or humming it while I was doing my homework so Mamaw or Daddy Jack wouldn't find out I was listening to the night demon.

That night I said my prayers to our Lord and Savior and told him I was sorry and wouldn't never go under the covers and listen to that demon station again. But after I got in bed, no other station was coming in, at least not with the thump. I twisted the knob a itty bitty bit, and then a little bit more. I turned the knob until I could hear the wolf creature howlin' and carryin' on about the music he called rock and roll. The music in those songs is almost always jumping and the words to 'em are wild and crazy and mostly don't make no sense. I kept listening every night 'til my heart would start racing too much and I'd have to turn it off.

The songs that get my heart beating super hard sometimes make my tallywhacker get all wiggledy which never happens except when I'm in the bathtub. Not only that, but every night another piece of my brain gets sucked out and a song gets stuck in there. This has been going on now for three weeks and two new batteries.

One night, the guy, who by now I realize actually calls himself "The Wolfman," played a song by Screamin' Jay Hawkins called "I Put a Spell on You." It was the most demoniac spooky sounding record you ever did hear and I had to turn it off right away. It scared me so bad that I didn't listen to any radio for two nights after that. Then there was a drought of thumpyness, and I snuck under the covers again.

Last Friday when I woke up I smelled bacon, which is the best way to wake up ever. I was coming down to have breakfast and I heard Mama humming. I heard her loud and clear. There was no mistaking it. Mama was humming "The Wanderer." I ran up the stairs and made a bunch of noise right quick so she would stop and I would not need to tell her about the demoniac radio or ask her how come she knows about the demoniac radio. I was panicking and my heart was racing. How did that song get in her head? Did she have her own demon radio under her covers and not tell nobody neither? Did the song eat through my brain and send radio waves out my ears after I was asleep and since it had already eaten mine, start in after her brain? Was my baby sister next? I had too much to think about and Mama was calling me to come eat breakfast and get my books ready for school.

All day I was worried sick. I had a hard time concentrating in class and Mrs. Whitehead got after me for daydreaming but I wasn't doing that at all! I was trying to figure out demoniac radio signals and that is tough work. That night after supper I didn't listen because I was too scared and did not want nobody in my family being demon possessed or going to hell. I barely slept a wink 'cause that radio was calling to me one minute and scaring me the next.

The next morning was Saturday and that meant bacon and pancakes and we might get to go someplace fun like the junk sale with Mama. I smelled the bacon and got up and heard Mama again humming in the kitchen. "The Wanderer" was still sucking away at her brain. I got real nervous and serious and started praying, "Lord, I don't want to go to hell and I'm super sorry ... but I really don't want my Mama to go to hell. So if you need somebody to go to hell on account of the Rock and Roll, you can send me instead. Mama is a good Christian Pennycostal and loves me and Jeanie. She works super hard to buy clothes and food and school stuff for us and helps me with my math homework. She always tells me to be kind and mind my manners because those things will carry me far. She does all this without no daddy around which I guess you already know. So, even if Mama did listen to the demoniac radio will you please, please, please forgive her? Amen."

I started to calm down and heard Mama call me to breakfast. She was still humming "The Wanderer." I didn't say a word. Then Jeanie came in and said, "What's that song, Mama?" Mama said she heard it on the jukebox at the Dairy Queen. "That thing really gets stuck in your head." Then she said she had a surprise for me and Jeanie, but we had to share. She made us both close our eyes while she pulled it out of the hall closet. It was a portable record player and sitting right there on the turntable was, you guessed it, "The Wanderer" by Dion and the Belmonts! She turned it on and put the needle down and played it all the way through. She started laughing and wiggling in her chair and sang along.

It hit me then and there that maybe, just maybe, I might be only partly Pennycostal, like Mama.

Listen to "Howlin'," from the album
For You to See the Stars by Radney Foster.

Sycamore Creek

She hung her church dress with reverent care on the branch of the live oak that God created as a coat hanger just for that occasion.

She flung her shoes and bra off as if they were completely insignificant. The dress was different. As she stood on tiptoe, in nothing but pale blue panties, to hang the dress just so, she revealed much more than her body. That dress was a symbol. Her heart and her soul were surely intertwined with her faith, but her body was about to become tangled up with mine in a gin-clear, gravel-bottomed swimming hole. She behaved as if that were as natural as lambs being born on my family's ranch in the spring.

She was blonde, Baptist, and curvy. Hollywood had recently fallen in love with all things skinny, but to me, and every shit-kicker high school boy with a Skoal can ring on the butt of his jeans, she was nothing short of stunning. In school, she tried hard to hide it by clutching her books close to her chest, wearing demure dresses her mother made from Simplicity patterns, but there was no concealing that figure.

She was whip smart and determined. Her name was Margaret but everyone at school called her Maggie. In our little West Texas town, that might as well have been the rest of the world.

Her daddy called her "Lucky." The youngest of seven sisters, she came along late, six years after her folks quit trying to have a boy. By that time, Maggie's daddy believed that God's plan for him was to have nothing but daughters. He took bets from all the fellas he worked with at the water company that the baby in his wife's belly would be a girl. The $380 he won paid for a few extras associated with her birth and started her college fund. She was born "Lucky."

I was baptized Robert Dean Whitmore but was never anything but Bobby Dean. My mother was Roman Catholic and my father grew up Methodist. Through some unspoken negotiation we had all become Episcopalians. A decade after my mother had died, I found out that she and my grandmother secretly had me baptized by a renegade Catholic priest in Schulenburg, Texas, just to cover all the bases.

My family had secrets, and we kept them well.

Maria Krueger was Mama's maiden name. Her father, Papa Fritz, of barrel chested German stock, descended from the immigrants who had first settled Central Texas when it still belonged to Mexico. His ancestors fought in the Texas Revolution. Fritz was strong and handsome and fell in love with a dark eyed beauty named Victoria Manuela Villanueva while he was working in the CCC labor camps in California. We called my grandmother Lita, short for *Abuelita*. Her nickname was the only part of my hidden Mexican heritage my father could not bury.

I loved the happiness and ease that I felt at Papa Fritz and Lita's home. I soaked up the sense of freedom there. My father never went with us on those trips to Schulenburg. As a small child, I assumed this was how all families operated. The older I got, the more aware I became of the dark rift between him and my mother's family. The only time my grandparents traveled west to our ranch was for Mama's funeral.

I don't remember learning to speak Spanish. I just spoke it the same way I spoke English. Every single human being who worked in our home or on the 12,000 acres we ranched was from Mexico. They spoke little, if any, English. There were two words for everything in my world. If I wanted to eat, sleep, ride a horse, play checkers, or skip rocks in the stock tank, I had better know how to say it in Spanish.

Our ranch had been in the family for many generations but in addition to ranching my father was a banker in town. He considered Spanish fluency an absolute necessity if one wanted to make a living. If speaking Spanish would help the bank make a loan, he was all for it. He spoke it to the hands on the ranch and Lupita our maid, fluently, jovially, gracefully even. Yet, I never remember him speaking Spanish to my mother. It was an unwritten rule that Spanish was not spoken between family members. We were white. Still, my mother spoke Spanish with me and my sisters when my father wasn't around. Putting me to bed when I was little, she would secretly whisper *mijo*, coo, and sing in Spanish 'til I fell asleep.

My father's bigotry was woven into the fabric of our family. My mother bore it silently. When I was a freshman at the University, it finally hit home. I had never heard the term "passing" 'til I got there but I knew what it meant the moment I heard it. My mother had been doing that very thing her whole life and in some ways, so had I.

Mama's name, Maria, would not have been an unusual name for a white girl named Krueger in Central Texas, it being both a Spanish and German name. She had raven black hair, piercing green eyes, and peach-colored skin. Her beauty could silence a room full of people merely by entering it. She had been a good student at the University, challenging, funny, with a sense of adventure. My father played baseball for the University of Texas and had been a bit of a hell-raiser. He was friendly and gregarious but my mother was not charmed at first. If my father was anything, he was doggedly persistent. I assumed that persistence and his infectious sense of humor was what won her over. They met in December of 1955 and the spring semester of 1956 turned into a whirlwind romance. In June, right after my father's graduation, they eloped and were married at the courthouse in Uvalde, Texas. Neither set of parents was happy.

My tendency to bust through fences like the headstrong goats on our ranch never served me well growing up. I didn't understand my father's prejudice as a child but I learned the hard way that speaking of it meant trouble. I have a vivid memory of picking myself up off the Saltillo tiles of our dining room floor, mouth bloody, jaw blasting with pain after shouting at the dinner table that I was just as Mexican as Rita Hernandez, my date that Saturday night. It was the only time I heard my mother cuss or speak Spanish to my father. He did not say a word as he left the room but his opinion was crystal clear.

When I was ten years old we had a ranch hand, Rogelio, who played guitar and sang. He loved *huapangos* and *rancheras*. I was so captivated by the sound that I begged him to play over and over again. He eventually put my hands to the guitar, patiently placing them into the shapes that make music, like a father would his child. When he headed back to Mexico, he left the guitar. That gut string filled an emptiness in me. It got up inside my soul and brought light and hue as if through a stained glass window.

By age twelve, I had earned enough doing extra ranch work to buy a beat-up Epiphone acoustic. I proceeded to learn every rock and roll and country song they played on the radio, especially what I heard late at night on XERF, "The Border Blaster." Two years later, my parents drove all the way to San Angelo to buy a brand new Fender Telecaster for my fourteenth birthday. I got my amp after the bank repossessed one from a guy in a college band and didn't know what to do with it. My father suggested they sell it to me on the cheap. It was the coolest thing he had ever done for me.

Maggie Walker insisted that we met in fifth grade, but I have no memory of it and that pissed her off to no end. In a way, I'd always known her like my family knew everybody in town. Her family had an account at the bank and like most folks had borrowed money from my father at one time or another. I do remember the night she and the Cauthorn sisters sang a rocked up version of "I Shall Not Be Moved" at the First Baptist Sunday night youth service. I was fifteen and backing them up on guitar. The sight and sound of her that night was forevermore burned into my brain. I never took the presence of Maggie Walker for granted again.

Our sophomore year, she shared a locker with my buddy Daryl Styles, a half a dozen down the hall from mine. I'd known Daryl since Cub Scouts. He was a monster piano player, who was even starting to write his own songs. Maggie and Daryl sang together at the youth services. One Sunday night they invited me to come play and sing with them.

Daryl and I formed a band over Christmas with the Russell brothers, and Tony Gutierrez. We called ourselves Pecos High Bridge. We played a few backyard parties that spring, and a 4-H dance where we even got paid. I always wanted Maggie to be a member of the band but her Baptist parents were never going to let her sing at a dance. She did sit in with us at one backyard BBQ, singing Linda Ronstadt's "You're No Good" and "Blue Bayou."

It blew everyone away.

That summer, I turned sixteen in late July, took the driving test, and passed with no fanfare. I'd been driving anything with wheels on the ranch for years. My parents were elated that I could finally run errands so they didn't have to go all the way to town over some forgotten item. Like any teenager, I was all too happy to oblige. Taking the long way home to hang out with friends was considered a fair swap.

The first afternoon I was allowed to take the truck to town alone, I noticed Maggie and her sister Miriam washing Miriam's Malibu in the 100 degree heat. It was a sight no boy could resist. I pulled into the drive. Miriam was older, a nurse at the hospital. She was always cool. She was brunette instead of blonde like Maggie. They shared the same smile, dry humor, and brains. Miriam loved a good conversation and especially an argument. She read books by Ken Kesey and J. D. Salinger, then passed them on to us, hoping we'd stir up shit at school. She wore stylish clothes she'd buy in San Antonio and Maggie and I both thought she was sophisticated, worldly wise.

Maggie's daddy drove up just as I was helping wipe the car dry. He teased me about getting my license. I asked if I could drive Maggie to the Sonic for a limeade.

"Lucky?" He turned to his youngest daughter and raised an eyebrow. She smiled and nodded her head. "Okay," he said, a little reluctantly. "Be home by suppertime."

That was the maiden voyage of me in a truck with a girl. I was high on my newfound freedom and we laughed all the way to the Sonic. It would never have been as much fun if it had been a real date. I would have been awkward and nervous. Instead, we cruised through town, eating tater tots, blasting "Born to Be Wild," while she played drums on the dash. I had spent the better part of six weeks on the ranch and Maggie and I had a lot of catching up to do. We talked about everything and nothing.

I had not a care in the world until she said David Bennett had asked her out to the movies on Saturday night. Although I told her he seemed like a cool guy, my burning face and silence betrayed me. I couldn't have explained my feelings to her. I couldn't explain them to myself. I had never been jealous before. As beautiful as she was, we were always "just friends."

I suddenly felt like turning for home.

Maggie and David dated most of our junior year, but broke up regularly. There was one spectacular scene in the school cafeteria when she threw a glass of iced tea all over him. I'm not sure what he did to deserve it, but he spewed a few choice words. The moment the word "bitch" left his lips, I flew over the table ready to cold cock him. John Wellworth beat me to it. After John landed that first punch, David fell into me, we splayed to the floor, and I pinned him. While he was struggling to get loose, I growled, "You should probably stay right here on the ground 'cause there's a line of guys ready to kick your ass, and they're gonna have to get behind me." Just as the dean of men and the football coach showed up, David told me to fuck off. That sealed his fate.

Wellworth and Bennett, both being on the football team, got a one-day suspension and had to run laps in full gear until they threw up. Nothing happened to me at all, which really pissed me off. It was as if I didn't matter. At least Miriam had the decency to ask me, "What the hell happened at school?" when Maggie wouldn't talk about it.

A couple days later, I bribed one of the ranch hands to buy me a six-pack of beer, which I secretly iced down in the toolbox in the back of my truck. Friday night, I drove slowly up to John after the game, hung the six-pack out the window, and made the hand off.

"Whitmore, how in the hell is it that you've been faster than me your whole damn life except the other day in the cafeteria?"

"We got a gig tomorrow night and I didn't want to hurt my hand." He laughed and handed me back a beer through the window.

On Monday, David Bennett walked up to me and said he had been out of line and didn't want any hard feelings. I wish I'd had a quick-witted comeback and have come up with several dozen over the years. My real answer was something to the effect of "we're cool," which has been eternally unsatisfying. That afternoon, I saw Maggie wearing his letter jacket and figured she must have put him up to the apology and that they were back together. Seeing him kiss her in the parking lot only confirmed it.

Music became my escape. From the library I checked out jazz and classical records. I was buying every rock and hippie country record I could get my hands on. Tony's mom was a big ranchera, conjunto, and mariachi fan and he and I learned the harmonies off her records. Those songs took me back to where I first started with Rogelio, a link to my hidden heritage. Singing a ranchera classic like "Las Mañanitas" could always be counted on to get me a couple free beers from the ranch hands on a Saturday night.

Maggie's folks made a huge concession and let David take her to the prom but she was not allowed to dance. Afterwards, they had to go to the midnight breakfast First Baptist put on so kids would stay out of trouble. I took Rhonda Montgomery. Her interest was elsewhere, and I was just trying to absorb all the cool parts the guitar player in the band was playing. She and John started dating shortly after that. I was happy for them both. David and Maggie finally broke up for good late that May.

Daryl, Maggie, and I sang three-part harmony Sunday nights at youth group. With Maggie free, all that summer we hung out at Daryl's, sang, and played. The excuse was to practice for Sunday but all we really wanted to do was be teenagers making music. It bound our friendship together as tight as our harmonies.

Daryl was a natural. One of those gifted musicians who could hear all the harmonies and every player's part. That's a rare thing in this world. He taught us to weave counter melodies and harmonies together in ways that made magic. I'd heard harmony in church my whole life and sung it in Pecos High Bridge. But when we sang Daryl's arrangement of "Oh Happy Day" in his folks' living room, leaning in close together, the hair stood up on the back of my neck. I'd fall asleep at night hearing that music in my head. Years later, working out vocal parts as Bonnie Raitt's bandleader I realized how much I owed Daryl, and driving up Topanga Canyon in LA late that night, I pulled the car over and cried.

Sunday afternoons belonged to me and Maggie. It wasn't planned. I just started picking her up early before youth group. We'd ride through town, sing harmony with the radio, gossip about school, talk about books and movies, discuss who really killed President Kennedy, argue Crosby, Stills, Nash, and Young versus the Eagles, and spill limeade and tater tots over whatever was funny. One afternoon while she was singing harmony to "Someday Soon," I turned off the radio. "You sing it."

"Hey! What are you doing? I love that song. Turn it back on."

"No, you sing it. I know you know all the words."

She looked at me over the top of her sunglasses as if I was an idiot, but she closed her eyes and sang. Hearing her a cappella was mysteriously sinful and holy. I figured out every way I could to trick her into doing it again. After awhile she would just close her eyes and start singing whenever we pulled up to the park across from First Baptist.

By the end of our junior year, the band was really tight. Robert Russell, our first drummer had graduated. We recruited Stevie McDavis who was only a sophomore but better anyway. Daryl and I traded off singing lead and harmony, Tony picking up the third when he could. The groove had that push and pull that made a girl's hips swing. Daryl's left hand on piano drove the rhythm and if we all paid attention to that, we could fill a dance floor. In West Texas, that counted as everything.

That summer, word got around about the band. We played every 4-H barn and hotel lounge from Del Rio to San Angelo. We even got hired by the Elks Lodge and made fifty bucks each.

My folks let us use their Waggoneer, pulling a horse trailer we cleaned up and lined with blankets for the gear. We played hard country, folk, and southern rock, but it had to have a beat. We unknowingly looked for whatever worked with the twang our Texas tongues were incapable of losing.

Daryl and I began writing songs together during the long drives home while the rest of the guys slept in the back. I'd drive and Daryl would write down lyrics and chord changes he'd figure out on my harmonica.

Half of writing songs is making shit up, the other half is telling the truth. You can only tell the truth you know, even if you only know seventeen years of life in a small town. If you are willing to share that innermost part—fear, love, a broken heart, you might end up with a song someone gives a damn about.

I loved writing with Daryl but he always held back. I didn't pry. Years of keeping secrets made me good at knowing when to leave people alone with theirs.

Maggie's musical gift was different than Daryl's. She was intuitive. She could feel where the emotion needed to swell or hold back. She felt the lyric in her soul, made you believe every word because she believed it. The same way she listened to the feel and emotion of a song, she listened to you as a friend.

Maggie was devout. She was never preachy, never put anybody down. She called herself Baptist if you asked, but her religion was walking down the street to ancient Mrs. Matthews's house, shelling purple hull peas, drinking sweet tea, and keeping her company. Her charity was the food boxes she put together at Christmastime. Her joy was singing hymns in harmony. Her righteousness was teaching the three Rodriguez children who lived in a trailer at the end of Wilsons Road how to read. Beto, the youngest, grew up to be a doctor. Her prayer was all day long when no one was looking.

Her grace was believing in me.

After Christmas break Daryl called me and said that he was grounded for at least a month. In typical Daryl fashion, he wouldn't talk about it. Something happened while they were visiting at his uncle's house in Dallas that pissed his folks off something fierce. The only thing he was allowed do was go to church, but his mom loved hearing Maggie and me sing gospel songs with him, so we could still come over to practice. Maybe she thought we were a good influence. However, if Daryl was grounded, so was Pecos High Bridge.

After three weeks, Daryl was toeing the line well enough that we were allowed to book a dance at Martin's Wool and Mohair Company over in Rocksprings for the end of February. Daryl still couldn't go anywhere. Singing with Maggie and me remained his only social outlet.

By then, we were all starting to think about college. Daryl applied to all kinds of crazy schools including NYU and Yale, but Baylor or Tech was about the best he could hope for. My lot in life was set in stone. I would be at UT, which was both my folks' alma mater. I was never even asked. Mama sent the application and that was that.

Maggie's college career had also been predestined, but she was secretly determined to change it. Her folks had her lined up to go to Mary Hardin-Baylor, an all-women's Baptist college. Maggie, however, had no desire to go to a school with nothing but girls. One night at the Sonic she looked down at her food and prayed, "Lord, thank you for this food and deliver me from that awful women's college. Amen."

She was set on going to Sul Ross State in the mountains of far West Texas. She had her sister Miriam, who had since moved out on her own, mail the application from her address so their parents wouldn't know.

We all kept secrets.

On the Saturdays we had an out-of-town gig I was in charge of circling by my bandmate's homes with the horse trailer to pick up them and their gear. I would stop at La Hacienda to get breakfast tacos for everyone and pick up Daryl first.

A deputy sheriff and a DPS officer were on the front porch talking to Mr. and Mrs. Styles when I pulled up. I got out of the truck slowly, sweating despite the cold. Daryl had left last night and not come home. The two cops drove away and I followed Daryl's parents inside. Mr. Styles was silent, staring out the window. His unease made me scared. Mrs. Styles said, "Bobby Dean, you should go pick up the other boys, then come back for Daryl last."

The tacos grew cold in the front seat, the news killing everyone's appetite. We swung back by Daryl's and loaded his Rhodes piano, on the outside chance he'd show up.

Stevie said we should kick Daryl out of the band. I spewed at him that when he started singing, doing arrangements, and could drive a backbeat as cool as Daryl, we would think about it. Until that time he could kiss my ass.

We rode the rest of the way in silence.

We set up the Rhodes but Daryl never showed. We bickered and fought through all four sets and never found the right groove. The dance floor was half empty and the manager shorted us 150 bucks. I got home at 4:00 a.m., exhausted but unable to sleep.

Mama was up. She had spent the day searching our ranch for any sign of Daryl. My father had to move a herd of sheep to the Double X pasture, but canceled his business meeting in Ozona to search at Mama's insistence 'til dark. Though it was obvious she had not slept, she made me breakfast and watched in silence as I ate.

At 5:00 a.m., my father came in showered, shaved, and dressed, but not in church clothes. He told me what they knew that I didn't. Daryl had had a terrible argument with his folks Friday night, taken his Dad's military issue .45 automatic, and driven off.

That morning, my father treated me like I was a man with a friend in trouble. "This is all probably going to be fine and blow over but the Styles are afraid that Daryl may try to hurt himself," he said. "I can only speculate, but whatever happened with him in Dallas over Christmas has turned that family inside out." There was a sadness and care to his voice, and a calm demeanor that told me I needed to keep it together. People might need me. I went upstairs, took a shower, and got dressed.

When I came down again Mama was on the phone with Maggie. She put me on the line. "Can you come get me?" Maggie asked. "I want to go look for Daryl."

"Hang on a second." I covered the phone with my hand and told my father what she'd asked.

"I'm not sure it's the best idea but I don't suppose you have much choice. Go on."

My father walked me out to the truck. "Son, don't be a hero. If you find Daryl, you call Sheriff Kusenberger. If he could be a danger to himself, he could be a danger to you and Maggie." He handed me a Long Nose .357 Magnum and told me to put it under the seat. I floored it into town to pick up Maggie.

It was Daryl's cousin who found the car about 8 o'clock that morning, driver side door open, on top of a hill overlooking Arroyo Seco. They found Daryl's body about fifty yards down the hill on a flat spot above the dry creek bed. He had shot himself through the right ear. It had gotten so cold that night, his head was frozen to the rock in blood.

We heard the news from my father when Maggie and I called to check in from the pay phone at Carter's Texaco. She ran and fell into the tall withered grass in the empty lot next to the station. She rocked back and forth on her knees, wailing, tears and spit streaming down her face. I bent down next to her, trying to get her up, but every time I touched her she hit me. Finally the numbing anguish and February wind took over. She let me lead her gently to the truck.

The news had already made it to Maggie's house. Miriam came running out and hugged her baby sister. The huge heaving sobs returned. As Miriam and her mom got Maggie into the house, Mr. Walker took me aside and told me that my parents were headed to the Styleses'. Mama had left me a change of clothes at John Wellworth's. "Half the town is already at the Styleses', son." No one was sure about the funeral yet. He thanked me and shook my hand. I noticed the tears beginning in his eyes, I ducked my head and said goodbye.

I drove to the Wellworths' and walked in the door without

knocking. This was a second home to me. John, sitting at the antique desk, looked up, said "Bobby Dean, this is way fucked up" and blew out a breath. I nodded. He said, "Your clothes are laid out on my bed."

John and I had walked through the neighborhood to the Styleses' as little boys in Cub Scout uniforms. Daryl's mama was our den mother. We knew every yard, every family, and the spooky house to avoid. We knew who played Monopoly, who played football, whose brother was a bully, and whose mom made the best cookies. We had been movie heroes with Hot Wheels and marbles in our pockets. The front porch where I first kissed a girl was a block away.

That day, we did not speak. We did not need to.

As we approached Daryl's, the winter sun, low in the sky, cast rose light on the gauntlet of mourners in the front yard. I said, "Oh, Lord," as the queasiness started. John read the situation and the dread on my face and made the best pulling guard play of his football career, blocking politely, weaving, apologizing, moving me forward until I was safe in the house.

But there was no safety in the house. Anger and grief hissed in my head the moment we were in the door. I was greeted by Charles and Todd, Daryl's older brothers, called home to grieve and for their mama to lean on. I looked around at the sea of sad friends and strangers and felt like my heart was going to explode. I could hear it pounding, the rhythm of it ringing in my ears. Everything started to spin and went black.

I woke up to the worried faces of Mama, Maggie, John, my sisters, and Mr. Styles. Dr. Klein was waving something under my nose. I felt stupid but I shouldn't have. Adrenaline, lack of food, and thirty hours without sleep mixed with grief is a powerful cocktail and I was no match for it. Mama drove me home and put me to bed.

I slept 'til noon the next day. Maggie's mother had called while I was asleep and asked if I was coming to town, could I come by? Maggie hadn't gone to school.

I drove to the Styleses' place first. I wanted to apologize. Mrs. Styles hugged me 'til I didn't know what to do. Mr. Styles put his hand on her shoulder and she let me go.

The funeral would be Wednesday.

Mrs. Styles asked, "Bobby Dean, Mr. Styles and I would like you to be a pallbearer ... if you're up to it."

"Yes, ma'am. I'd be honored."

"Would you and Maggie sing 'In the Garden?'" Fighting back tears she talked about how she'd loved hearing Maggie and me singing in the living room with Daryl. My chest ached.

Grief had already knocked me on my ass. The last thing in the world I wanted to do was disappoint this stricken mother but I didn't know if I could pull it off.

"I think so, Ma'am, but I'll have to ask Maggie first."

Maggie was sitting wrapped in a quilt on her front porch. She didn't move as I parked the truck.

Miriam, home from her shift at the hospital, came out, hugged me, kissed my cheek, and thanked me for coming. She sobbed in the still of the winter afternoon, pointed at Maggie, and went back in the house.

"Hey Maggie." I tried to put my hand on her shoulder but she jerked away.

I walked into the house behind Miriam. "Is she talking at all?"

"Not really."

Mrs. Walker had made chocolate cake. I took two pieces out to Maggie and sat down next to her. "Who said you could sit here?" she spat out.

"Nobody ... your mama handed me two pieces of cake and I didn't want to eat 'em both." She turned and stared at the sunset. "I hate cake. I hate you. I hate Daryl ... and everybody and everything living or dead."

"I know ... it's kicking my ass, too."

She whispered, "Don't you dare cuss in front of me, not now."

I shut up and waited.

The desire to be free of Mrs. Styles's request pushed me. "Maggie, Mrs. Styles wants us to sing 'In the Garden' at Daryl's funeral." I looked her straight in the eye. "I'm not sure if I can keep it together."

She stared at me for the longest time. "Say that again?" I said, "I'm not sure if I can keep it together."

"No! No, before that."

"Mrs. Styles wants us to sing 'In the Garden' at Daryl's funeral." I watched the light slowly come back in her eyes and watched it warm her whole body. "Yes," she said. "We have to." She took both of my hands and put them on her face. "We have to, for Daryl." Her lower lip quivered. She struggled to get out, "It's the best thing we have to give him … it's the only thing we have left." She slumped her head over into my lap, crying.

The quiet was broken by a Mexican blackbird in the distance. "We wouldn't have it to give if it weren't for him," I whispered from the bottom of my throat. She laid there, curled up in that blanket 'til suppertime. Holding her gave me the strength to sing at the funeral—for Daryl, for his family, but mostly, for Maggie.

We only ran the song down a few times. Maggie would be singing a different part without Daryl. We changed the key. We worked the harmony to bring tension to just the right notes and figured out how much to slow down, adding length to the entrances of each chorus. Pausing as we held the "and" in harmony.

And … He walks with me
And he talks with me
And he tells me I am his own

As I packed up my guitar, Maggie looked at me, tears welling in her eyes, and said, "What we just did with that song? We owe that to Daryl."

Something about a waltz is sadder than songs in 4/4 time. Your heart beats in 4/4. It helps you find your rhythm. Maybe that's the reason three-quarter time can feel so sad. It's bumping against your heartbeat, not with it, unsettling, yet comforting.

The church was filled to overflowing, because of tragedy but also because of love. As Maggie and I sang, the collective tears of family, friends, a church, and a small town poured out in anguish. I wanted to believe that if Daryl had known how much he was loved, felt the light in that church, he would never have pulled that trigger.

Darkness lies, convincing you that no one loves you, that no one could, that love does not exist. But on that cloudy, cold winter day, the light won. We loved each other through grief, through complications unspoken. It is harder to judge the sin of suicide if you have baked cookies for or wiped the nose of the boy in the casket. Sorrow becomes stronger than judgment.

When the service was over Daryl's brothers, cousins, and I carried that heavy box to the hearse. Riding to the cemetery they told stories about Daryl when they were kids. I was grateful to sit in silence and soak up their memories.

I helped seat the family under the tent and carry Daryl's body to the gravesite. I don't remember what Reverend Bradshaw said or what the youth choir sang.

As they were about to lower his casket, I shouted, "Wait!" My father looked at me with anger for making a scene. But the Styles family only stared curiously at me. I told Mr. and Mrs. Styles I had something Daryl would need to take with him and I showed them my harmonica. I told them about Daryl and me writing songs, driving back from gigs. "I'm sorry for interrupting the service."

Tears began to run down Mrs. Styles's face. She smiled and reached up to hug me. Mr. Styles put his hand on my shoulder. "Would it be alright if I kept it? It would mean a lot to me."

I handed him the harmonica.

After Daryl's body was lowered into the ground, the family, then others, threw handfuls of dirt in the grave. The band had decided that we would all throw a handful in together but a handful was not enough. I saw a shovel leaning against a backhoe behind a hedge, grabbed it, and started shoveling. The groundskeeper gently put his hand on my arm. But I shook him off so strongly that the back of my hand smacked his chest. He walked away. Only Daryl's brother Charles, Maggie, Miriam, and my family remained. My father came up to me and said it was time to head home. "With all due respect, sir, I'm perfectly capable of getting myself home."

"I believe you are, son."

Charles said, "Bobby Dean, you shovel as long as you need to." And then walked away.

Maggie and Miriam sat on folding chairs for more than an hour while I shoveled. Finally spent, covered in sweat despite the cold, I dropped the shovel.

The next day I woke up with a fever and sore throat. By late afternoon, my fever was raging. Mama took me to town to see Dr. Klein who said it was the flu. I wove in and out of violent chills and fever for six days. I had the recurring nightmare of executing Daryl on that rock above Arroyo Seco with a .45 automatic, making him get on his knees before I pulled the trigger. I'd wake screaming, burning, freezing.

On my first morning back at school I saw Maggie in the hall. We were strangely awkward with each other. John and I snuck out for lunch to get an honest to God cheeseburger. I saw Tony and he asked how I was doing. We talked about nothing 'til he brought up the band. "Tony, I don't even know where to start with that … not yet."

I was on autopilot at school, wrestling with sorrow. Kids steered clear of me, including Maggie. John Wellworth let nothing shake him. He'd hang with me in silence or leave me alone, listen to me rage at the radio for no reason and called me on my bullshit when I barked at a sophomore girl trying to tell me how sorry she was about Daryl.

Spring break, to the rest of the world, is about time off from school, taking a vacation with your family, or raising hell with your buddies at the beach. For ranchers, particularly ones who raise sheep and goats, it's about work. Dozens of lambs and kids were being born on our ranch every day as we were rounding up for shearing.

John had packed his saddle and rig in my truck on Friday. He was coming to the ranch to work. He was an excellent horseman and I'm sure my father paid him well. He would be my roommate for nine days, right when I needed a friend. I'd like to think that thought was not lost on my parents.

Food during roundup and shearing was of spices hand ground in a *molcajete*, roux and sauces made in exacting order, prayed over while being made and before being eaten, recipes in my mother's heart, passed down generations and being passed down again. Normally, the hands cooked their own food in the bunkhouse, and at any other shearing the shearers would be in charge of their own food as well, being given protein on the hoof as part of the contract. My mother would have no such thing. She was the cook. It only took one of her meals to win any argument. My mother, my sisters, and Lupita took charge of three squares for the shearing captain, eight shearers, extra hands, the regular crew, our family, and a few other folks from town who were in the know.

During shearing, my mother made food that mere mortals could only dream of, food reserved for the gods. If you were blessed, she would ask you to help. In return you would get what we called a "*bocado*," a little mouthful to taste. John Wellworth would have worked half a day free for one of those. The last night, once the ranch was sheared, there was always a fiesta.

One evening as the sun was setting, John and I were putting away a second helping of *cabrito* when he swallowed a mouthful and said, "You don't have to understand it."

"What?"

"You don't have to understand what Daryl did. It's eatin' at you. I mean, hell ... it's eatin' at all of us ... but you more than the rest of us." I didn't respond, didn't know how. "Plus, it's making you a pain in the ass. We haven't even snuck any beer from the hands." He laughed. I walked over to Enriqué, leaned in, and said, *"Amigo, dame dos cervezas a escondidas."* Enriqué smiled, leaned around the corner to see if my father was around, pulled two beers out of a washtub full of ice, handed them to me, and made a motion with his hand, "down low to the ground."

John and I walked towards the west pasture. The sun was down, the horizon glowing red. I popped a can and took a long sip. "I don't know what to tell you," I said. He let that sit. "In my mind I understand what happened and in my heart I know suicide is the darkest lie ever ... but I can't figure anything out ... I wake up feeling like a bull ran over me." John looked up at the first stars coming out. "You are gonna feel like crap for a while, we all do. But you gotta start talking. I mean shit ... I had to talk you into stealing two beers to get you to talk about it." I laughed. He took a swallow. "But, if you don't talk about it at all? That craziness will start rolling around in you and that darkest lie you talked about starts looking pretty believable. I don't care who you talk to ... me, your mom, Maggie, Father Mills, Reverend Bradshaw or even," he raised his eyebrows, "your dad?" I cracked up. I smiled and nodded with my hands in the air to surrender.

We stomped the beer cans flat. I said, "Thanks, I know I've been a pain in the ass."

"No kiddin'. I've been here six nights and you have yet to pick up a guitar. Dumbass!" He made a basket into the trash with his crushed can, threw his arm around my neck, and pulled my head over, "Now, where the hell's your Spanish guitar?"

Years later, after my mother died, he and I drank a beer watching the sun set in that same pasture.

As I was trying to sleep that night, I realized I'd been avoiding Maggie since the funeral. I called her the next morning. Her mother answered, said she was in San Antonio with Miriam but would be back tomorrow evening.

"Ma'am, would it be alright if Maggie came to a party Saturday night? My family always has one at the end of roundup."

"Well, Bobby Dean, I think that'd be just fine if she wants to. I'll have her call you when she gets home."

It was warm, so we sheared into the night under the lights.

At 5:15 a.m. the next morning, sore, sleepy and hungry, Mama handed me and John half-coffee, half-Mexican hot chocolate, and pointed us toward the table on the back patio filled with eggs with pork chile verde, refried beans, roasted tomatoes, crumbled cotija cheese, orange slices, and fresh tortillas. Even after stuffing our bellies, we would be starving by noon. We were two mouthfuls into breakfast when my father came through the back door and called out, "¿Listos? You're burning daylight." There were still hundreds of sheep to shear.

My father worked as hard as anyone on the ranch. Growing up, I'd watch him do a chore and then he'd do it with me 'til I got it right. After that I was expected to do it myself. He could be so patient when you were learning, a loving teacher. It was hard to reconcile that caring man with the anger I also knew.

My father didn't drink a lot. As far as I know he was not unfaithful to my mother. He could be tender and fun loving to us kids. It was not just prejudice that made his anger rise to strike like a viper but anything that painted outside the lines he'd drawn. Love across society's racial lines, women in places of authority, or a career in something he perceived as bohemian were all as dangerous as a drunk driver or a feral pig. Punishment was swift, sure, violent. I used to wonder if he felt hoodwinked by my mother. Had she hidden her nationality from him until after they were married? The family myth was Mama was the German-Texas girl my father fell for in college. Searching past that tale was dangerous. Keeping my mother's heritage a secret was the first wall to the prison he built around his soul.

Mama left me a note on the kitchen door that Maggie was coming to the party with her sister. She signed it with the question. "*¿Te gusta?*" ("Do you like her?") I was not sure if I knew the answer. When she asked if I got the note, I said, "yes ma'am" and kept moving. I heard her chuckle as I left the room.

We had sheared the last of the herd by early Saturday afternoon. Friends from town were already arriving. Some were there to help Mama with cooking, some to just sneak a taste and drink on the porch. Our house had a wide, expansive back porch and patio, with the bunkhouse, corrals, and barn visible across the way. Daddy had built Mama a stone outdoor kitchen with a grill, griddle, barbecue pit, wood oven, and spit. It was alway busy during roundup but on the last day my mother conducted an orchestra of cooks.

I had my back to the door when Maggie walked in. The sight of her stopped my mother in her tracks. She quickly caught herself. "Maggie! Come in." I turned the moment Mama spoke and saw what made her pause. Maggie had cut her hair and was wearing a new dress with a shorter skirt than usual and a scooped neckline that just barely showed cleavage. There was a sophistication about her, class. She was gorgeous.

Holding a pan full of guacamole, I stood frozen with my mouth open. Lupita took the pan from me and said, "*Cierra la boca y salúdala.*" ("Shut your mouth and say hello to her.") Both sisters giggled. "Hey, Maggie," I said slowly. I didn't know what to do next. She took the lead, hugged me, then pulled back to look at me and said, "It's good to see you."

We got iced tea and I showed her around headquarters. Once we got away from the crowd, it was the same old Maggie. Free with her smile, easy to talk to, bright eyed and full of questions about the ranch. Then it was my turn. "Ok, that dress? Your hair?"

"Miriam took me to San Antonio for my birthday, just me and her." My shoulders slumped, "Your birthday."

"Shhhh," she put her finger to my lips. "We've had a lot more on our minds than birthdays." We made more small talk about San Antonio. I finally spoke the unspoken.

"I'm really sorry I've been avoiding you these last few weeks." I swallowed hard, "I know it's crazy but the thing of it is ... when I see you, I can't help but see Daryl." Her eyes glistened. "I know. It's been the same for me." She stopped walking, "Bobby Dean, it's always gonna hurt. I've had two best friends in this world, you and Daryl. I've already lost one of them and I don't want losing him to rob me of ... you." I sucked in a breath between my teeth. "I'm sorry, Maggie. I don't want to lose you either." I smiled and crooked my arm so she would take it, and we walked toward the house. "Now let's go eat some of my Mama's cooking. Oh, by the way you have to sing for your supper."

The hands wore their best that night. Two weeks before, my mother had slipped them extra money to get new clothes for the fiesta but told them she had better not see any of it before the party. Tonight, she doted on each one of them, said how handsome they looked and met a few of their *novias* who had come from town. The hands mostly stayed to themselves and ate by a campfire in front of the bunkhouse, the barrier of language and legal status being a river too far to cross. The exception was our foreman Ruben and his family. Though the divide between Anglos and Latinos was wide, they gathered at the party tables like everyone else. Ruben's daughter Déborah, who was two years behind us in school, interrogated Maggie and Miriam about San Antonio. A few other prominent Mexican American families who were business friends of my father's were there. Ten years earlier they would never have been invited.

The feast was Mexican and German rolled in a century and a half of Texas ranching culture. *Cabrito, chiles rellenos, carne guisada,* two kinds of homemade tamales, *jeagerschnitzel, frijoles a la charra,* handmade smoked venison and pork sausage, *calabacita,* sweet and sour red cabbage, roasted garlic potatoes, green beans with tomatoes and onions, all of which was served with homemade guacamole, *salsa picosa*, *pico de gallo*, and hand-pressed corn and flour tortillas fresh off the *comal* and for dessert, a pan of flan the size of the hood of my truck.

As amazing as the food was, my favorite part of the night came after the meal. We circled the chairs on the porch and instruments began to come out. The hands all moved our direction. Where music was concerned, there were no barriers. My father's friend James Lockhart was there with an old Martin triple ought guitar. Tony borrowed my Epiphone and a ranch hand, Rolando, had a button accordion in the key of C. He was pretty good and could cover anything in C or G. I used Rogelio's guitar he had left me all those years ago. Mama made me start. I tore into "Tiger by the Tail." Mr. Lockhart went next with "Long Black Veil." Folks were having small conversations over the music until Maggie and I started singing harmony on "she walks these hills…." It got church quiet.

Applause thundered as we finished. I asked Rolando in Spanish if he sang. He said no but knew lots of songs instrumentally. We both knew "Jalisco" and kicked it off. *Gritos* and cheers rang through the night. I told Maggie she had to take a turn. Tony and I knew a half dozen songs we could back her up on from the band but she looked at me and said, "Just a Closer Walk with Thee." She sang angelically but with the blues in her soul. Her voice broke perfectly on "grant it Jesus is my plea."

We sang and played into the night. Mama let me know it was time to end when she quietly said, "Cucurrucucú Paloma," her favorite song. Maggie didn't speak Spanish except for a few words and phrases remembered from school, but when the chorus came around she sang harmony phonetically. Mama looked at her as if she were a miracle.

As the party broke up, I walked Miriam and Maggie to their car. Maggie kissed my cheek and said, "This was so wonderful." I stood staring at the taillights as they pulled away.

Monday at school, Tony, James, and Stevie wanted to talk

about getting the band back together. They'd been jamming as a trio over the last month. There was a junior, Kiki Hernandez, who played piano and Farfissa organ. They wanted to ask him to join. I slowly shook my head. "Guys, I ain't ready for this. I just ... I don't ... know what else to say." Stevie, looking like he was fighting back tears said, "Daryl was our bandmate, man, and a cool friend to all of us but you two ... were like brothers." He had been looking down but he lifted his head and looked me square in the eye and continued, "I'm able to play drums because of Daryl, because he convinced y'all ... I could do it. I wouldn't be here talking if it weren't for him, but the only way I get to make music is if I'm in a band ... that plays somewhere."

He had a point.

Tony said they all thought I might say no but wanted to give me the chance. He swallowed hard, "We won't use the name Pecos High Bridge ... out of respect for Daryl ... and you." Stevie scuffed his boot on the ground, looked up at me again.

"If you ever want to sit in, I'll split my share with you any time."

I picked up Maggie one Sunday in late April. She had several pieces of sheet music in an old shape notes hymnal. I flicked at the sheets and said, "What are those for?"

"Hiding my future."

She had used the hymnal to hide two acceptance letters, one from Mary-Hardin and the other from Sul Ross. "I'm not sure you can pull that off much longer." I shook my head, "Just be honest with your folks, tell them what you want to do."

"Are you kidding me? My mama and daddy are hard-shell Baptists and I am the most Baptist girl they have ever raised. They have been wanting to send a daughter to Mary Hardin-Baylor since Moses ran for President! I am the last daughter! This is it! Last chance Texaco!" When we both stopped laughing, I asked, "Moses ran for President?" She giggled. "It's in the Bible, look it up."

"Maggie, pretend I'm your folks and tell me why you want to go to Sul Ross." She thought for a block and a half. "One, my two best friends have been guys and there are none of those at Mary Hardin. Two, Sul Ross is much less expensive than Mary Hardin and I can go there for the first two years and get the basic courses done. After that I can decide to finish there or go to another school and not be in debt or a burden to my parents. Three, I'd be closer to home and I like it in Alpine with the mountains and Big Bend. It's beautiful."

"And it ain't so damned hot," I added.

"Don't cuss around me." She winked.

"So, you are telling me that you can't explain to your folks that you want to save them money, be closer to them, and you like the mountains? Maggie … really? Just do it. They're not going to have some big blow up if you show them you thought this hard about it. It's not like my folks."

"Your folks are great."

I didn't respond, just kept driving.

We headed out of town fifteen miles before I pulled up to a gate with a lock. I spooled the combination.

"Where are we going? Is this on y'all's ranch?"

"It's actually on the Knapp place but it borders ours. It's a pretty spot on Sycamore Creek. They let me fish here, camp with Daryl and John." Saying Daryl's name in present tense stung. We rattled along then parked about twenty yards above a gravel pool, clear green and blue, eight feet deep just below a riffle. It was shaded by a large live oak with Spanish moss on the cut bank side, and a half a dozen sycamores on the gravel bank. She jumped out of the truck. "This is beautiful."

"Nobody knows about it 'cept us and the Knapps. I'd like to keep it that way. Otherwise that lock would be cut off every weekend and it'd be full of trash."

Maggie had already slipped off her shoes and rolled up her jeans to dangle her feet in the water. I picked up rocks and skipped them while she took in the beauty of the place.

"Maggie ... you need to be thankful that you can talk to your mama and daddy. I'm jealous. I can talk pretty well to my mother, but my father is another story. I don't think I've ever had an honest conversation with him in my life."

"Why?" she asked, puzzled.

"It's a very long story." I swallowed hard. I needed to tell her but didn't know why. I listened to the water, "Here's the short version."

I skipped a rock, picked up another and stood there, killing time to find courage. "My grandmother was from Mexico, which makes my mother half Mexican and me and my sisters part Mexican as well. There is something about it that eats at my father so much it's never talked about." I skipped another rock. "I think he is scared it will make us second-class citizens. All that hiding ... messes up your head. Ya know?"

She got up and looked at me, "Bobby Dean, nobody cares about that and God's never cared about it. What difference does it make?"

"It made a difference when I was five and got backhanded. I'd said I was Mexican, like Nana Lita, my grandmother."

She waited, shocked.

"That is my oldest memory of my father." I hunted for another skipping stone. My back was to her. She walked up, touched my left shoulder, and by the time I'd turned around her arms were around my waist, head down, buried in my chest. Her tears were soaking my shirt but she made no sound out of reverence for my confession. Finally, she whispered, "Bobby Dean, I love you. No little boy deserves to be hit that way." We stood there like that no telling how long. "That's not the only time, is it?" she asked. I shook my head and she groaned in response. "I don't have any answers Bobby Dean but I do have prayers and somehow ... God has an answer."

I twisted out of her arms. "God damn it! I can't hear that

right now. I don't even know if God exists but if he does, he is one cruel son of a bitch." She did not move as I raged. "If he's really out there, why would he give me a father that beat the shit out of me and is so bigoted he's terrified someone might find out my mother's Mexican? I'm Mexican!" I started to cry for the first time since Daryl had died and whispered, "Why would He let Daryl twist around whatever pain was in his mind so far that he blew his brains out?" I slumped to the ground. Her voice was quiet and calm and while there was anger behind it, there was no malice. "You're not the only one hurting. You're not the only one who has had bad things happen to you and you are definitely not the only one carrying around secrets.

"There's something you don't know about Daryl," she said. "He was gay. He told me last year, swore me to secrecy. He was terrified of anyone finding out." She turned away. "A week before he died, he told me what happened in Dallas. His parents caught him making out with another boy, and they were ready to throw him out 'til he apologized, lied, and said he was drunk ... didn't know what came over him.

"I've run through it a million times ... all the things I could have done, or said, to keep him from killing himself. I was the only one he confided in ... I let him down. So, no! You're not the only one with a cross to bear."

I was trying desperately to wade through the flood of information. "Daryl was a queer?"

"It's called 'gay' these days, Bobby Dean."

"I know what it's called but ... but I mean he never acted ... that way. Never!"

She sighed and shook her head, "Being gay or queer or whatever you want to call it doesn't make you act a certain way. Besides, how would you expect him to act out here in redneck world?" She wiped her tears. "Bobby Dean, you and he are the two best friends I've ever had, and with the possible exception of John Wellworth, Daryl was your best friend. Does him being gay change any of that? Does it make you less sad about him being gone?"

I hung my head, listened to the water gurgle, and said, "No." My mind was reeling. There are many things I wished I'd asked her that day about Daryl but I didn't.

It would take me a long time to come to terms with knowing Daryl was gay. That resolution was hampered by his suicide. My acceptance and a fresh set of tears came years later, sharing a bottle of wine with Maggie after a gig late one night in New Orleans.

On that afternoon, all I said was, "I need to get you home."

Two days later Maggie spoke to her folks and she began making plans to go to Sul Ross. Those last weeks of our senior year were lazy. My teachers could not have cared less whether I took my exams. There were lots of parties and I saw Maggie at most of them and the senior functions over at the Baptist church.

That emotional afternoon on Sycamore Creek put something between us, something I couldn't put my finger on. The raw pain and doubts shared that day hurt but sealed an unspoken vow to keep each other's secrets.

Graduation day is always full of mixed emotions. Everyone is excited about where they are headed but wanting to hang on to the bonds of high school friendship. I couldn't foresee that I would eventually lose touch with all of those people except John Wellworth and Maggie. The moment of silence for Daryl was the stark reminder that I had lost one friendship forever and in that silence I became determined never to lose Maggie's.

Before the ceremony, Maggie came over and said, "I told my folks I might eat dinner with you tonight if you didn't have plans." I don't believe I'd ever smiled as big. "Sure, you pick."

"Sherman's Steakhouse, but I'll pay. I've been saving up."

"Nope, I'm kind of old-fashioned about that."

"I didn't do this so you would buy me a steak!" she protested.

"I know. I'm just sad that I didn't think of it. Time to celebrate!"

After we threw our caps in the air, I drove us to Sherman's at the edge of town.

It took me over a decade to realize the significance of being able to say what you really feel to another human being, particularly one as honest and beautiful as Maggie. We sat and talked 'til they closed down. As I walked her to her door the only thing that felt right was to kiss her. We kissed a long time.

I called her the next evening and had hell shooing my sisters from behind the kitchen door. Kissing Maggie had changed everything, and nothing. We talked a long time, then she said, "There's a special service for graduating seniors at church this Sunday. Would you come with me and my family? I think they'll do something to honor Daryl. I know his folks will be there."

"I'll be there, too, come hell or high water. I know … Don't cuss in front of you."

I could hear her laughter as she hung up.

That Sunday, standing in the shade of a huge magnolia in 90 degree heat, Maggie stood in a blue and yellow floral print dress, scooped low in the back with a thin white shawl to cover her shoulders. I have yet to figure out how someone could look that sexy in a church dress.

Rev. Bradshaw's words that day were empty. He talked about Daryl without talking about him at all. He never mentioned the struggle, depression, guilt, hurt, and anger that we were all going through. Knowing what Maggie had revealed to me at Sycamore Creek made it even more hollow. Maggie's cheeks burned. We could not wait to get out of there. When she asked me to come to Sunday dinner at her folks right after the service ended, it was a weight off my shoulders. Her folks would not pry nor preach. Like Maggie, they just loved.

After Mrs. Walker's fine southern Sunday cooking, Maggie came up to me as I was talking to her dad and said, "Take me for a ride in your truck." Her father looked at me, looked at her, and said, "I long ago quit trying to argue with this one, you better do like she says."

"Yes, sir."

We went to the Sonic for a limeade and by that time it was hotter than hellfire. She said, "Let's go to that pretty place on Sycamore Creek."

I pulled up above the swimming hole. We sat without speaking, the sound of cool running water our only company. She leaned over and gave me a kiss. I kissed her back. She slid closer, curled her feet under her legs, and kissed me more passionately. She put her forehead against mine and proclaimed, "Bobby Dean Whitmore, I'm going skinny dippin' in that pool down there and if you don't join me I will never speak to you again." She jumped out of the truck, kicked off her shoes, giggling, unsnapped her bra, pulled it through the armhole of her dress, and flung it aside. I didn't know that such a feat was possible.

By the time I was out of the truck she was hanging that dress on a branch, as if it were sacred.

She tiptoed like a tightrope walker down to the water so as not to get a stone bruise, slipped off her panties, and splashed into the water. I followed as best I could, trying to take off my starched shirt, fumbling with my belt buckle, and pulling off my boots at the same time. Gravity won. Maggie howled with laughter. Down to my boxers, I realized I had a flagpole attached to my hips and was completely mortified.

She laughed, "Are you embarrassed or just shy because of that erection?"

I turned twelve shades of red but sassed back, "I'll have you know that in West Texas that is known as a 'hard on' and I have never seen a girl naked before."

"It's just natural, it's not like you can help it. Besides, Bobby Dean, I am not a girl, I'm a woman." She floated on her back and teased, "Does this look like a girl to you?" I lost my drawers and dove into the pool.

The cool water calmed my inflammation as I swam over to her. She back paddled and darted and laughed, eventually letting me catch her by the sycamore bank. She was standing, her breasts floating level with the water and we kissed again. We kept kissing, my hands discovering her body and hers mine 'til she shoved my chest and I fell back into the water. She exclaimed, "You! Have to go over to that side of the pool for a little while."

"How do you know I'll stay over there?"

She stiffened and said in a low voice, "Because you are a gentleman ... and you love me ... and I asked."

I was horrified that I'd said the wrong thing, scared her. "You're right, Maggie, on every count. I would never do anything you ... don't want to or ... or hurt you in any way." I was breathing hard, "I didn't really ... come prepared for this. I'm still not sure what's happening or what to do, but," I caught my breath and smiled, "I like it." She laughed.

We talked and swam and made out 'til the burdens I carried floated away in the current. At one point I asked, "Why don't you apply late to Saint Ed's or ACC? We can sing together, then you can transfer to the University. You wouldn't have any trouble getting in UT."

"I'm not moving to Austin. Besides you're not gonna last more than two years in college. You'll be playing in bars or touring with somebody famous ... writing hit songs."

"How do you know?"

"Bobby Dean, music is in you and it ain't ever letting go."

"But why don't you come sing with me?" I swam closer and kissed her neck.

She pushed me away. "I do love to sing with you and until right now it was the most special thing I get to do with you. In a way ... it still is. Anyway, I already had the chance when y'all wanted me to join Pecos High Bridge." She swam away to the other side. "Can you see me riding in a van with a bunch of sweaty, stinky guys all over the country, each of 'em thinkin' about gettin' in my pants? It's not going to happen! Look, Bobby Dean, it's not my dream … I don't want it that bad … but you do. And you should because you're the only person I know who is that good. Besides," she splashed me, "can't a girl have her own dreams?"

She swam over to a place with soft pea gravel on the sycamore bank and laid down half in and half out of the water.

I swam closer to her. "Why are you doing this?"

She smiled, "I knew this would happen with someone in my life … I didn't want to look back and it never have been with you." She kissed me hard and pulled back, "Don't overthink this like you do most things, Bobby Dean." She curled her head under and laid it in the crook of my shoulder and began kissing my neck. She whispered, "I'm not gonna let you fuck me. I'm not ready for that and the truth is neither are you."

"You … You are cussing?"

She giggled, kissed my lower lip, and teased, "I know the words, Bobby Dean, I just choose not to use 'em."

I pulled her to me with a deep kiss as we laid side by side. She slowly and carefully took my hand and guided it between her legs. "Just barely brush your fingers there," she whispered, out of breath. "Not too much, just gently," she sighed. She moved her fingers to teach mine, which became slicker as I kissed her lips, neck, and breasts. After a few minutes she began to stroke and caress my loins. She moved more and more and eventually we weren't really kissing as much as breathing with our lips barely touching. As we writhed in time together she clutched my back with her hand underneath my arm, then shuddered in waves a few times, cried out, and bit my chest. I could not help but come as well.

She laid her head on my chest, both of us breathing hard. After a few minutes she began to sob and I held her. Her crying was neither sad nor happy but something else altogether. It was powerful. I would want it my entire life.

We laid there breathing slowly in time. She got up and dove

in the water breaking the spell. We swam, talked, laughed, and kissed but something was different between us.

The shadows grew longer. We gathered our clothes and dripped dry in the arid heat. The sun low in the sky, we awkwardly, shyly, got dressed.

There are times I wonder, lying awake at night, what would have happened if Daryl had not killed himself. Would my relationship to Maggie have been different? I wish he could have felt how much we all loved him and not pulled that trigger. I miss him all the time. I believe to my soul that God put the three of us together to make music. If for no other reason, so that Maggie and I would have each other as a comfort.

When we were dressed, she kissed me. She said, "Look, you are leaving here and you're gonna chase something very special. Don't let what anyone else says keep you from trying to make music, Bobby Dean. People will tell you you're a fool on a fool's errand. When they do, remember me right here, telling you this right now. You can do it, Bobby Dean. You were born to."

Then she kissed me again.

Listen to "Sycamore Creek," from the album
For You to See the Stars by Radney Foster.

ACKNOWLEDGMENTS

It takes a lot of folks to write and publish a book. I could never have done this without the help of all these crazy, art-chasing souls. You all inspire me in so many ways.

To Cyndi my amazing wife who has always encouraged me to stretch my vision and chase my dreams. You put up with me, love me, inspire me. You're the glue that keeps our family together. You believed in me and told me I could do this knowing it would only take time away from us. I love you.

To my beautiful children, Julien, Jackson, and Maureen, you make me remember to take life head-on. Your enthusiasm is infectious. I love you.

To my friend and writer Judy O'Brien, who called me a son-of-a-bitch after she read my first story. It is my favorite compliment. You walked me through so many doubts. You then called, cajoled, and encouraged everyone you could think of who might help me get this book out. I love you for it and can never thank you enough.

To my friend Gardiner O'Kain, thank you for your discussions and advice about ethnic and racial identity in literary characters. I'm so thankful for your counsel. Much love.

To my old friend Déborah Hernández-Salinas, thank you for editing my Spanish … and the great posole recipe.

To my brother writer Darden Smith, you drove me to pursue every way of storytelling I could and your soulful advice helped give me the courage to do this.

To Judy Richards, thank you for your soft guidance and patient editing of this book. It and I are better for it. I cannot wait to hug your neck.

To Eric Erdman, who made me laugh, write music, and build fires at Working Title Farm. You are an incredible musician and were a welcome distraction. To late night lyrics, heartfelt tears, and your honest opinions. Cheers! Plus, you alone can drive Shari crazier than I can.

To Cary Smith, thank you for the amazing artwork.

To Kerry Brooks at River's Edge Media, thank you for this opportunity and for keeping all the numbers and minutia straight.

Thanks also to Alice Randall, Ann Shaw, and Eddie Heinzelman for opening doors and encouraging this path.

To my publisher, editor, and friend Shari Smith. You are a force of nature and are true with both a compliment and a correction. You are bighearted, generous, hard working, and leave no stone unturned. You opened your home and heart to me and my clan. My favorite working moment remains the night you told me, "Radney! If I wrote that line in a song you would kick my ass." You were right. I am proud to call myself a Working Title Farmer. Thank you.

CPSIA information can be obtained
at www.ICGtesting.com
Printed in the USA
LVHW04s0905060818
586105LV00002B/269/P

9 781940 595658